Also by AJ Kaynatma

AJ Kaynatma >>his Traumatic Brain Injury

*AJ Kaynatma Morphed into Sonnet Form
& a Smattering of Other Various Poetry*

Numbers Don't Lie …But Can They?

T.B.I. Confessions

You Can Very Well Be A Jack Of All Trades But A Master Of None.

MAN ON A MISSION

A.J. KAYNATMA

Copyright © 2019, A.J. Kaynatma
All rights reserved.
Cover image used under license from Depositphotos.
No part of this book may be used or reproduced in any manner whatsoever without written permission except in the case of brief quotations embodied in critical articles and reviews. Requests for authorization should be addressed to: turkishajk@gmail.com.

Cover design by Ivica Jandrijevic
Interior layout and design by www.writingnights.org
Book preparation by Chad Robertson

ISBN: 978-167-4740072
LIBRARY OF CONGRESS CATALOGING-IN-PUBLICATION DATA:
NAMES: Kaynatma, Altan Javit, author
TITLE: Man on a Mission – A Genius's Cognitive Up & Down Tale / A.J, Kaynatma
DESCRIPTION: Independently Published, 2019
IDENTIFIERS: ISBN 9781674740072 (Perfect bound) |
SUBJECTS: | Fiction | Romance | Dating | Mathematics |
CLASSIFICATION: Pending
LC record pending

Independently Published
Printed in the United States of America.
Printed on acid-free paper.

24 23 22 21 20 19 8 7 6 5 4 3 2 1

DEDICATION

I write this book in honor of my younger brother, Bertan Kaynatma. He's an inspiration to me. For many years, pre-accident, I was always the brain of the Kaynatma children. Now post-accident, I learned that he's simultaneously teaching college classes & pursuing his PhD—all in the distant, foreign country of Turkey. Way to eclipse my gargantuan shadow, bro!

"Never give up, and be confident in what you do. There may be tough times, but the difficulties which you face will make you more determined to achieve your objectives and to win against all the odds."

—Marta, Brazilian footballer

CONTENTS

ALSO BY AJ KAYNATMA	ii
DEDICATION	v
EPIGRAPH	vi
CONTENTS	vii
FOREWORD	xi
PRE-amble	xvii
ACKNOWLEDGEMENTS	xix
Event Full Back Story	1
Rustlin' up the Kindling	3
The First Cut Is the Deepest	9
New Approach?	13
Faith in New Places	17
Give a Lil'. Take a Lot	20
Narrow the Search	22
Good Work Takes Time	24
Trial and Error	27
Game On	30
Husband Love or Friend Help?	33
Numero Uno	35

If, at First, You Don't Succeed, Try, Try Again	39
Romance in God's House?	41
Romantic Appeteasers Aside	46
Know Your Surroundings	48
Try Something New	50
New (Not Always) = Good	53
So Far, So Good	57
Trial by Fire	59
Good Score? Bad Score?	62
Does the End Justify the Means?	65
Inner Questioning	67
Too Much of a Bad Thing?	69
Square in the Circle Hole	72
Set 'em Up. Knock 'em Down	77
Why Change a Good Thing?	78
Confirmation Needed	81
Better than Pizza?	84
Worry?!	87
Dust Yourself off, and Try Again	89
Confidence Is Key	92
Dirty Feelings	95
Natural Pick Me Up	98
Psychological Rights >> Physical Wrongs	103
Retrieval	106
Good Things Come to Those Who Wait	111

Mind Changer	115
Shared Interests	120
New Service	127
Oh, Sweet Irony	129
Swim Before Eat	132
Misunderstanding Resolved	136
For the Kids	139
Gotta Talk It Out	144
The Juice Is Well worth the Squeeze	146
Show Appreciation	149
Two Peas in a Pod	153
Numbers Talk?	161
Musical Trigger?	164
Other Commitments	166
Excessive Happiness	169
There in Spirit	172
Lasting Effect	176
Afterword	179

FOREWORD

AJ was an anomaly, in all the best ways, before his accident at age 23. More than eleven years later, he is still an anomaly but in very different ways. AJ's brain is unique, so his TBI is unique.

The reader should know something about AJ as a child and a young man, pre-accident. His personality was slightly different then. He had many reasons to brag but he NEVER did. He was confident in himself but he didn't boast about it; he just did what he needed to do, and was almost always successful. He was competitive because he was obsessed with numbers, and still is. He was very self-motivated, driven to succeed in all he did. He was also a social animal: he would organize a bunch of people to play kickball, to have a party, to go to a sports event, to play trivia at a local bar, to do anything! He was very active. He mentions in his first book many of his accomplishments, academic and athletic; these are generally accurate. But again, pre-accident AJ would never brag about them. Also, he was funny and prone to practical jokes.

ACCORDING TO AJ'S SIBLINGS

His sister, Jeyda, 8 years younger, said AJ was "always" an older brother-type. Always teaching her relevant life lessons like campfire songs he learned in Boy Scouts. You know, along the lines of, "Hi. My name is Joe, and I work in a button factory. I've got a wife and a dog and a family..." It has a certain rhythm to it. He often imparted brotherly words of wisdom such as, "You can pick your friends. You can pick your nose. But you can't pick your friend's nose." He much preferred being goofy to any brotherly mentorship. He begrudgingly checked over her Math Superstars extra credit assignments, for example, but was the first to stick out his tongue from across the dinner table when no one else was looking.

His younger brother, Bertan, recalls a few choice stories. He said:

> AJ liked toilet humor (and still does). Once when I was driving someone else's car in the rain, AJ was in the back and a friend was in the front passenger seat. I was having trouble seeing out of the rear window. Somewhat anxiously I asked "Is there a rear wiper?" In return, a right hand was proffered from the back seat, coming through the center console, with AJ helpfully explaining, "I have my rear wiper right here," as if the hand he used to wipe his ass would be any use at the time. He always said this stuff with a grin on his face, not smarmy-like.
>
> AJ was addicted to sports, and even as kids, bad weather or lack of equipment and/or appropriate playing space, never stopped him. Once, when we were quite young, maybe 6 and 8, we decided to play some baseball, in the house. All we had was a baseball bat, but neither a ball nor appropriate playing space; it didn't stop AJ. (I followed his lead.) We had to stay inside, and the closest thing to a ball happened to be a balloon, and the closest thing to an outfield fence turned out to be our nearly floor to ceiling living room window. We soon discovered that, no matter how hard you hit a balloon, it doesn't travel far. This only encourages our inexperienced minds to hit it harder. I took a swing, and then handed it to AJ. In his defense, I believe his grip had not caught up with his arm strength, so as a result, he swung the bat, hit the balloon, and sent the bat flying out of his hands. It crashed straight through the enormous living room window and out into the front yard, leaving a cannonball-shaped hole in its wake. Not knowing what to do, I ran through the house in a panic, perhaps looking for a place to hide. At least it wasn't my fault.

> A good example of AJ's antics is when he trapped his flatulence in a car full of people and locked all the windows. OR, I remember AJ's trapping ....
>
> I always remember when we played neighborhood football; AJ was the sweatiest guy, and the hardest to tackle.
>
> AJ is the king of nicknames. For me: Bert (from Bert and Ernie), Bertrum Grover Weeks (the movie, *Sandlot*), Bear, Bertrominator, Bartholomew, and just recently, Berry Berry Boisenberry. (He's still got it!) As pledgemaster of the fraternity at his university, AJ nicknamed approximately 25 pledges for the year, 2006-07.
>
> Post-accident: he is really funny, witty, and language savvy. Boastful, it appears, but he explains that behavior as the need to prove himself. Still self-motivated and determined to succeed. Still stubborn. Often demanding and easily frustrated, as he copes with a growing ability to understand his own situation.

For context, AJ was previously known to quote a lot of movies, to recite sports stats, to excel in mental math, to use very correct grammar and good vocabulary. He can still do all of those things but might forget a conversation you had with him an hour ago.

AJ doesn't remember the accident or the first several years afterwards. The brain protects us from trauma that way. He stayed at three different hospitals before he went to the long-term rehab facility, 200 miles from home, where he lived for three years. We rented a trailer home outside the nearby town that whole time. AJ's best friend from childhood, Grant, and his girlfriend, L. stayed there, alternating weeks, for the first year, while I communicated with family and friends across the globe about AJ's challenges and achievements through an online blog. AJ's support system included his brother Bertan, who was in college; sister Jeyda, who was in high school, and my best friends, Grant's parents. Everyone took turns visiting on the weekends. Someone was almost always there with AJ.

When AJ got to the long-term facility at the end of October 2008, he literally couldn't open his mouth because the spasticity clamped it shut. He was barely able to respond to yes/no questions with a thumbs up. He could sit in a wheelchair, with support, but only for a short time. They used a Hoyer lift to transfer him from chair to and from his bed. He had a feeding tube from the beginning and still does. AJ struggled through three kinds of grueling therapy (physical therapy, occupational therapy, and speech therapy) every day, five days a week, for three years. He never refused to do what a therapist wanted him to do, even though he could barely move ANY of his OWN BODY by himself. The two-time black belt Karate Kid could not roll over. I had to leave his therapy sessions many times because my heart broke to see his struggle. Yet, he never indicated he wanted to stop trying.

Almost three and a half years post-accident, AJ moved into his own house, closer to family and friends. This was possible because of a legal settlement with the tire company. (The cause of the accident was a defective, 9-year-old tire that shredded on the highway.) He has caregivers 24/7, and two nurses for tube feeding. He's in a wheelchair most of the time, but he's working hard to walk at a special gym, with a walker and minimal assistance. AJ uses a spelling board to express himself. This is a homemade template of the QWERTY keyboard. He points to every letter of every word to spell out his thoughts, using complete sentences. AJ is now making progress using oral speech, but he is still very hard to understand.

An observer can see the physical damage. The cognitive damage, however, is a mystery. It's easy to notice that he still has way-above average intelligence in several areas (especially math and vocabulary), an outrageous sense of humor and a very quick wit. BUT, there are significant deficits in his memory, processing abilities, perception, and judgment that are not so apparent. Neither is his limited emotional capacity. In fact, these are very hidden issues. These "hidden issues" are the direct result of his unique brain injury.

Please IMAGINE the reality of the aforementioned deficits. It is ESSENTIAL to keep these in mind when you're reading his book. His memory deficits are both long and short term so there are some inaccuracies in his story. His perception is often skewed or different from reality.

It's important to know something about his girlfriend, the love of his life. They dated for eight months before the accident. She stayed with him for almost four years AFTER the accident. She didn't just visit him, she STAYED with him. In the beginning, she often slept overnight at the hospital; later, she spent every other week at the long-term rehab facility, 3 hours away; and finally, she lived with him in his new home for over a year. She tried to do everything to make their home as "normal" as possible. She had caregivers during the day only; she did all the rest of his care, including tube feeding, every night and all weekend. (She was studying to be a nurse at the same time.) Eventually she had to break away, depressed (that it would never be "normal") and worn out. You will read how AJ perceived her departure.

I have read a few books about TBI survivors, but those were written by fully recovered individuals, friends, or relatives of someone with a TBI, or ghostwriters. AJ has NOT RECOVERED from the diffuse axonal brain injury that he suffered eleven years ago. His brain is operating at much less than its prior, exceptional capacity. Yet, he wrote his memoirs in his first book, *AJ >> his Traumatic Brain Injury*. (Beware!)

AJ Kaynatma—Morphed into Sonnet Form is his second book, with many more to come!

Numbers Do Not Lie ... But Can They? is AJ's 3rd book but his first attempt at fiction.

T.B.I. Confessions is, in AJ's own words, "various confessions from the inner workings of a startlingly still very genius-like TBI (traumatic brain injury) victim."

Man on a Mission is AJ's 5th book. It is semi-autobiographical.

His "voice" as he will explain, is evident in the way he writes. He cannot use his own, actual voice to emphasize what he wants to emphasize, so he uses a number of capital letters. He has several other idiosyncratic means to punctuate his writing, and some other peculiarities sprinkled in. But, it's all him! Bear with it— you will be fascinated!

This is HIS story, as HE perceived it.

Martha Kaynatma (Mom)
Davie, FL
Oct. 2019

PRE-AMBLE

I wrote this book after re watching—for like the umpteenth time—a particular genre of film. The story style and edge of my seat plot twists kept me glued to the screen! I was inspired.

I cannot lie; this novel is semi-autobiographical with an entertaining (I hope) twist of fun fiction![1] I've always been a man of irrefutable fact. I frowned on fictitious tales. I considered them lies. As a devout, left brained logic seeker, I spent my first 23.2438 years breathing—on my own[2]—aboard Earth, rolling my eyes and chuckling at the scientific absurdity of the fiction genre. but then hell froze over.

I was in a devastating car accident. As I worked to rehabilitate my brain and my limbs, I noticed:

While limiting my leg propelled movement, my resulting traumatic brain injury enigmatically stimulated my creative synapses. Thus, I'll definitely exaggerate when the opportunity arises.

Since my traumatic brain injury also triggered my extreme organizational tendencies, I've separated my writing into an exorbitant # of chapters.

Sooo, I'd characterize my work as fiction with a non-fictional base. I speak in semi third person, referring to "Alex" as the protagonist.

Yes, the term, genius, is very hopeful and a bit egotistical. But, I kinda need that self-aggrandizement to maintain my optimistic view of life. I aim to show the extreme low from which A.J. 2.0 began. He now

---

[1] Besides, I've already written my memoirs, *A.J. Kaynatma >> Traumatic Brain Injury*.
[2] Outside the womb

embraces his enigmatic nature and flourishes as a proud weirdo … as A.J. 3.0! A.J. 3.0 is definitely more socially aware and a better decision maker than both A.J. and A.J. 2.0.

A.J. 3.0 is supremely self-confident. He likes to refer to himself in the third person in an attempt to—seemingly—minimize his bias and maximize his objectivity.

ACKNOWLEDGEMENTS

I should thank my friends, my teachers & my coaches in high school for constantly motivating me to succeed—no matter how bleak the circumstances may appear.

EVENT FULL BACK STORY

Alex Kalatovski's spectacular early life overflowed with both mental and physical accomplishments. He earned perfect scores on his math S.A.T. and S.A.T. II Math Level 2. He was his high school's valedictorian (4.7613 GPA) at a very prestigious college preparatory institution. He applied to and was accepted into just one college. Ivy League Harvard university. Or—as he soon developed a Bostonian accent: *Hahvuhd Yahd*. He successfully graduated in four years, while remaining an active member of both the school wrestling team and a fraternity. Balance of business (academics) with pleasure (wrestling). He maintained a 3.26 GPA in an accelerated program at a graduate level business school. He dropped the class after about 1.33 years of studies. It proved to be just too much work in not enough time. As hard as he tried, Alex just couldn't sufficiently allocate his weekly awake time between four hours of martial arts teaching, six hours of martial arts learning, forty-five-plus hours of work as an operations manager for a petroleum distributor, and six hours of business class. He figured:

That's a required minimum of fifty-five weekly work hours plus about four preferred weekend hours to socialize divided by ~126 weekly awake hours = ~46.83%. Without the completely optional business class, and no more social life, I could decrease that down to ~37.12%. That'd now be 49 weekly required hours[3] /~132 weekly awake hours.

---

[3] Alex considers his martial arts participation an obligation, 'cuz he's trained for thirty-six years. Plus, he feels committed to the education of the children he's teaching.

In lieu of this time management, Alex decided to change jobs. He sought something a lil' more enjoyable and applicable to his everyday life. So, he became a film critic.

Aside from being cognitively enigmatic, he is very athletically gifted. Alex has taught karate and jujitsu for close to twenty-seven years[4]. He's earned two *nidan's*[5] in '*shuri ryū karate* and '*shōrei ryū*' *karate* and one *shodan*[6] in *shindō yōshin ryū jujitsu*. Additionally, he participated in youth gymnastics to increase his flexibility.

Granted, he could never do a full straddle split. But, he got pretty damn close. He quarterbacked his high school football team. His senior year, he even led the team to a state championship! He played community basketball and organized soccer—separately—for three seasons. Up until his junior year of high school, Alex wrestled great. But, then, at sixteen—when he won the state tournament—he became a great wrestler. There's an exorbitant difference!

Extracurricular wise, he'd constantly play football, ping pong, "*Beirut*"[7], drunken tee ball and swim with friends.

---

[4] He's trained in assorted martial arts for over 36 years.
[5] 2nd degree black belt rank
[6] 1st degree black belt rank
[7] Fancy name for beer pong. Actual beer pong uses paddles. Like ping pong. Hence the name.

Rustlin' up the Kindling

As a direct result of his athletic dominance, Alex's social livelihood greatly increased. His gridiron success and routine magnificence on the wrestling mat granted him access to the jock clique. He was sorely disappointed to learn how accurate the unfortunate stereotype is. That athletes—generally—have very few topics they can discuss intelligently and extensively beyond their respective sport.

Conversely, excelling in all aspects of academia in a highly reputable college preparatory school only distanced himself from all non-nerds. Sooooo, he self-segregated himself from ~91.54% of his graduating class. (465 out of 508).

Alex hoped to alter many views, when he eventually attended his high school class's 25-year reunion festivities at a local performing arts center. Even as a young man in school, Alex was determined to bridge the conversational gap between varsity lettermen and asthmatic dweebs. Alex earned the school distinction as a scholar athlete. That way, he better united the glasses-wearing, homework-seeking, snorting twerps with the muscle-bulging, adoration-craving, flexing competitors.

"Why can't I be both?" he exclaimed. "I'll pose that question to the nerds. The circular reasoning is probably over the heads of you, kinetically gifted," Alex deduced.

Brandon Whitfield—the big, muscular jock: "Hey, I resemble that remark!"

Alex: "Touché, buddy! P.S. touché is French. Here, touché is a fencing term. And, fencing is a sport. Sooo, now…" Like WWE'S The Rock. "Do ya smeeeeeeeh duhbuh duhbuh eeeeehlll … what the rock is cookin?!"

Brandon: "Oooh! Respect! Nice reference." He snaps his right thumb and middle finger, as he thrusts his right hand forward.

Alex: "Okay, so nooow you respect me?! Question: Why did you enjoy and respect professional wrestling so much but put down amateur wrestlers … such as myself?"

Brandon: "… Um, well, you rolled around with and grabbed other guys. I didn't know whether to hide my sister or my brother from you! Sicko."

Alex: (several deep and audible exhalations) "Other than the pigskin, scoring and timing, how is my wrestling different from your football?!"

Brandon: "Well, one: we have padding. So, we can hit each other harder."

Alex: "Correction. You wear padding, 'Cuz you're all a bunch of panzees. … I wouldn't be surprised to see a football trainer running out onto the playing field for an emergency—to give the tight end a maxi pad."

Brandon: "Hey. I was the tight end."

Alex: "… Jeez., how appropriate! Say we've got a game on Friday. How's your flow?! Actually, don't tell me. TMI. Speaking of which, you—as a football player—play games. I—as a wrestler—participate in matches. Wrestling is a metaphor for life: there are pushes and pulls, ups and downs, winners and losers. There are no timeouts. No water breaks. It's not a game!"

Brandon: "Two! Wrestling gets two halftimes! Football only gets one!"

Alex: "First of all. Careful of your wording. How could we have two halftimes? What math are you in?! And, they're called intermissions. They each last all of about a hundred and eighty seconds. That's three minutes. Secondly, action wise, there are three 2-minute periods, as opposed to four 12-minute quarters."

Brandon: "Okay, fine. What's your wrestling stage name?"

Alex: "'Stage name'?! Uuuuum, my last name. Amateur wrestlers don't have stage names, 'Cuz it is an actual sport. Unlike your beloved WWE, which the name itself indicates is not real: world wrestling entertainment."

Brandon: "Uuum. Well. Uuuuum. You're pissing me off. I'll kick your ass!"

Alex: "C'mon, dude. You're better than that. Use your wooords."

Brandon: "So, you want me to beat you up, then insult you more? Jeez, man. You're crazy."

Alex: "Yeah, crazy like a fox!"

Brandon: "Okay. You're a fox, and I'm a hunter ... with a gun."

Brandon cocks his right fist, high and back.

Alex: (audible sigh) "I'm giving you imagery for how I am more cunning than you."

Brandon: "Whatever, loser."

Alex shrugs his shoulders.

Alex: "You were warned."

Brandon steps in with his right foot and hurls a right-handed hook punch at Alex's head.

Alex: "Bad move." Alex side steps away from punch—to his own right and thrusts up a left-handed *shuto uke*[8] to block the punch. Alex grabs and secures Brandon's right wrist with his own left hand and rotates his own body more or less 90 degrees counterclockwise—to his own left. Alex swings his own right arm under and around Brandon's approximately horizontal right arm.

Alex sarcastically mutters to Brandon: "Excuse me, hunter. Is this

---

[8] Knife hand block in Japanese.

your gun?" And then chuckles.

Alex leans back and falls—gracefully and deliberately—backwards. As he falls, Alex rotates his own trunk slightly counterclockwise to semi tug Brandon over and to land on his own left side. Rather than landing on his back, which may knock the wind out of him, Alex uses his extensive martial arts training to think to avoid just plopping.

Brandon called upon his football drills to know to roll, as he fell. Alex—still clasping Brandon's right arm—sits up and rotates his own trunk counterclockwise and slides his own right leg around Brandon's right bicep to fully ensnare Brandon's right arm between his two thighs. Alex presses his own thighs together as he slooooowly upwardly eases his own hips.

Brandon: "Ow, ow, ouch!"

Alex: "Now, if you don't want me to break your arm, just repeat after me: 'I, Brandon Gallegos, …'"

Brandon: "I, Brandon Gallegos, …"

Alex: "'… promise to respect wrestlers and to stop being a dick to them, …'"

Brandon: "'… promise to respect wrestlers and to stop being a dick to 'em …"

Alex: "'… 'cuz I'm scared of them.'"

Brandon: "Hell naw! That's a lie!"

Alex arches his back and thrusts his own hips up more, as he pulls Brandon's right wrist down, intensifying the secluded pain in Brandon's hyperextended right elbow.

Brandon fights back tears and stammers: "Okay, okay! 'Cuz I'm terrified of 'em!"

Alex: "Nice synonym!" He releases Brandon's arm and sits up.

"Now, that was called a *juji kitame*. I could have busted up your arm sumthin' nasty! But, I didn't. Why?!"

Brandon mumbles under his breath: "Dick."

Alex: "'Cuz unlike you, I am not a dick. I respect all. Ya see, if I were like you, and I chose to flex my strength over all those less athletically gifted, I'd be constantly lookin' over my shoulder, wary of karma's vengeful eye. It's a bitch! Isn't it better—from all respects—to show respect and kindness to your peers and elders than to demand fear?! Oh, that reminds me your birthday's in July, right? Well, as the anniversary of my escape from my mother's womb was in March I am your elder."

Brandon stretches his right arm. "Where the hell did you learn to bend someone's arm like that?! Jeeeez! And, when?!"

Alex: "Well, I began my martial arts training at the tender age of seven. Approximately thirty-six years ago. I've earned three black belts—in two similar but different styles of karate—and one in jujitsu—or, ground fighting to the layperson. To you."

Brandon: "Jeez, ha ha! You were even a dork in there for all those years! Ha ha ha! And, again, when might you have accumulated such valuable body control?!"

Alex: (audible sigh) "Did my *juji kitame* teach you nothing?! Don't belittle those of whom you know nothing. Ignorance is not bliss. Also, FYI, the term, dork, originated in 1950s British army slang, and it means penis. Through the years, dork is sometimes used in reference to a whale's penis, specifically. What that implies about size, I know not." He chuckles.

I'd practice two weekday evenings a week, every Saturday and Sunday morning and teach kids' classes twice a week. So, I'd attend your occasional soirees. Just, with me, I had wisdom."

Brandon: "Sooo, if you were there and not drinking, ... how'd I not beat your ass?!

Alex: (audible sigh) "Three issues of concern:

1. I can drink alcohol and not get drunk. It's the science of my maintaining a 3-way balance among a 6'1", 197-pound frame, fluid intake, imbibing speed and metabolic output.

2. 'Tis infinitely better to be socially approachable without "drinkin' beers and kickin' ass." As you often like to yell.

And 3) did you learn nothing from the *juji kitame?*"

Brandon: "Whoa! You know how to ... Not get drunk? Would it work for a ... 230-pound guy?"

Alex: "Does a bear shit in the woods?"

Brandon has a confused look on his face.

Brandon: "Hhhmmm. What about polar bears in Antarctica?!"

Alex: (exasperated) "Arctic forests. I'm sayin' that science rules all. I know we attended a Catholic high school. But, did you honestly believe all that religious what have you they were spewin'?! Ya think I captained our championship football team with unbeatable talent?! Hellz naw! Thanks to our athletic scouts, I watched a lotta game film of our opponents, learned defensive backs' tendencies, wrote notes and exploited them."

Brandon temporarily leaves to get a pen and paper.

Alex: "Soooo, to respond to your ridicule. Yes, I do tend to slouch, when I'm at rest. And, yes, I am attracted to female genitalia. However, according to my extensive anatomic studies, I am, in fact, not a phallic representation of the male reproductive system!"

Brandon: "Hhhmmm. A whale's shlong?! Noice! Now, I wAnna be a dork!

Alex excitedly thought—to himself: *My first conversion!*

THE FIRST CUT IS THE DEEPEST

After all that talking, Alex's throat felt a bit dry. So, he wandered over to the concessions area to grab a drink. He strolled up to the beverage table, where he casually waited in line behind three people.

Alex ponders internally: *How can I make a joke about my up and down past. That makes me more appealing?*

Behind Alex, Brandon and a woman soon joined him in line. Brandon taps Alex on the shoulder. He turns around.

Brandon: "Dude, this is my wife, Lisa. She's a language arts teacher at the local high school. … honey, this is Alex. Watch what you say around this guy! He was our valedictorian. So, don't ask him any stupid questions."

Alex: "There are no stupid questions. There are only stupid people. Ergo, …"

Lisa—to Brandon: "Heeey! Honey. What are you implying about my questions?!"

Alex—at the head of the concessions line: "'Garçon'?!"

A female fellow alumnus answers his service summons.

Alex: Oh! Pardon me for implying that you're male. I just wanted to ssseeeeem sophisticated by using a foreign language. Damn French!"

Maria—the waitress: "Doesn't my face nullify the male 'garçon' confusion?!"

Maria bats her eyes at Alex.

Alex: "I don't know what I could say to defend my egotistical stupidity! So, I'll just shut up."

Maria giggles. "Ooooo kay. Then, how are you gonna get my attention?"

Alex: "Watch and learn."

Alex steps back … away from the concessions stand. He steps up to the table. He raises his right index finger, as if to ask a question in class. He stammers: "Uuum, excuse me? Uuuum, I tip well?!"

Maria giggles. "Um, you do know there's no tipping here, right?"

Alex: "Pppssshhhttt! Details. Details. Just! Lemme do my thang!" Again, he raises his right index finger and politely hollers, "Excuse me, waitress?"

Maria wipes off the counter and greets him, exasperated: "Yeah, what do you want now?!"

Alex: "No, no, no. No! Is that how you address everyone?! You've gotta remain in character!"

Maria audibly sighs and tries again: "Yes, sir! You look … thirsty! … What can I get for ya?"

Alex: "Wowza! What lovely service! In honor of my delightful server. Lemme get a slippery nipple. And a glass of cranberry juice."

Maria: "Cranberry juice?! What, ya got a U.T.I.?!" (she giggles.)

Alex: "Negative. I just like to occasionally clean the pipes … with juice, not with manual self-pleasure! Eeewww! I very much appreciate your concern, though."

Maria steps away to grab the drink ingredients. She quickly returns with sambuca, Bailey's, two glasses and ocean spray. She pours about a half ounce of Irish Cream into a glass. She leans for the sambuca.

Alex: "Wait, wait, wait, … wait! I'm sure you already knew and were just testing me. But, you've gotta pour the sambuca first, … before the Irish cream, 'cuz of their differing densities." Alex pushes up his glasses.

Maria: "Oooh! Thanks. I forgot just how smart you are!

Alex: (half-jokingly) "Let's start with a glass of my cranberry juice. No mixing! Easy enough."

Maria pours a glass ¾ full of cranberry juice. She hands it to Alex. Then, she grabs the sambuca.

"Thanks a lot, … smarty!"

After the sambuca, Maria adds some Irish cream. Alex downs half the cranberry juice and gives Maria a thumbs up sign.

Alex: "Okay, enough of this charade! I just wanted the cranberry juice to drink. My Slippery Nipple request was my pathetic attempt at flirting."

Maria: (rolling her eyes) "Well, you're right. That was pathetic."

Alex: "Maria, how 'bout an 'A' for the effort? Can I get your number?"

Maria: "Well, you can get it. As in, you are physically able to get it. But, if I do not give it to you, then, technically, you may not have it." She smiles big and slyly hands Alex a crumpled-up piece of paper. Alex smiles back and puts the paper in his jacket pocket—without reading it.

Alex pays for the drink and steps away. Maria moves on to the next customer. Alex shrugs it off. He turns around to see Brandon's snickering.

Brandon: "Ha ha ha! Priceless wordplay with the drink! It's as if you reeeally ordered a Kamikaze! Ha ha ha! Lisa, babe, any of your friends single?"

Alex: "And wAnna mingle?! I'm embarrassingly desperate."

Eeeeerie awkward silence.

Brandon: "Pardon me, hun! Lisa, this is Alex, the ol' school valedictorian and state champ quarterback."

Alex: "I was also a state champion wrestler."

Brandon: "Ssshhh! Be quiet about that! We don't discuss questionably homosexual activity." He turns to Lisa. "His apologies, hun."

Alex slaps the back of Brandon's head. "Dude! What'd I tell you about respecting wrestlers?! Also, might you have mentioned my *juji kitame* on you?"

Lisa looks quizzingly and earnestly at her husband. "What what?!"

Brandon: (begrudgingly) "Fine. Plus, Alex was a state champion wrestler ... with two bla ..."

Alex: "Three!"

Brandon: "My bad! Three black belts in karate."

Alex: "And jujitsu."

Brandon: "Jeez, dude! Stop listing your accomplishments to me! I'm not gonna date you! Bummer for you, but I'm taken."

Lisa: "By me!" She leans over and kisses Brandon on the lips.

Alex: "Ya see?! Scenes like this—Brandon's kissy face with assorted girls—helped me cut weight for wrestling. Uuuggghhh!"

Lisa: "'Assorted girls'?! What the hell?!"

Brandon: "Relax, babe! I ended up marrying the best."

New Approach?

Alex continued to shmooze at his reunion. Many of his chums—from his high school days—were now married.

"Congratulations! I'm very happy for you!" he'd all too frequently outwardly exclaim. But, inside, Alex was a steaming cauldron of jealous spite. So, in this particular instance, bein' social was—ironically—not healthy for Alex's frail psyche.

As Alex wandered aimlessly around the reception area, the hired band played Yes's hit song, *Owner of A Lonely Heart*. Alex rolls his eyes and mutters, "Oh, sweet irony!"

Thoroughly exasperated, Alex unleashed an expletive laden protest, as he flailed his arms in disgust. He was utterly perplexed at the band's piss poor song selection.

However, Alex's misunderstood air thwacking was well received by many a guest. Some people interpreted the heavy heaving as head banging gestures. Others saw his gesticulations as dance moves for hard rock. Still more peers viewed 'em as dramatic interpretations of long-sought love. He threw in a few pelvic thrusts[9].

Over the generous cheers, Alex palmed a fiver to the band leader, as he requested a different song. Next, the musical group selected Rachel

---

[9] A "pelvic thrust" is a folkstyle wrestling takedown attempt in which the attacker suddenly pushes his own hips forward—into the lower body of his opponent—as leverage, while muscling him down with his upper body.

Platten's *Fight Song*.

Fantastic pick thought Alex. He shadow boxed the air. 'Twas evident Alex possessed fighting skills, as his bobbing and weaving allowed him to sneak by every single one of nobody's punches. However, Alex also displayed his semi questionable judgment, when he decided to ... again, just shadow box—without any contact—spar against a rather buxom female's chest. After ducking and dodging a few, Alex acted as if the woman's right breast floored him with a sneaky hook, and his tumble ended the meeting.

Continuing with the reclusive theme, the band next played, *YOLO* (You Only Live Once) by—the semi-appropriately named group—Lonely Island. Alex rolled his eyes and chuckled at the band's song selection. He made a scene, as he spazzed out—with himself—for the entirety of the song before he retired to the beverage area.

Alex debated attempting to flirt with Maria again. But, she looked uber busy at the concessions booth. He wasn't feelin' the song the band was now playing, so he sat down. Alone. Alex internally, non-visibly cried.

"These were my peeps! I was a state champ football QB and state champ wrestler! Don't they mean anything to anyone?!"

Alex's internal voice of reason interjected: "Dude, you're livin' in the past! Absolutely no one gives two shits what you did. ... A quarter of a century ago! Highlight the now!"

Almost as if the band read Alex's mind, they started blasting, *Something There* from *Beauty and The Beast*. Alex sat—by himself—and counted prime numbers, as he tends to do as a worst-case scenario. Sensing his unhappiness, Brandon and his wife ventured over to talk.

Brandon: "Buddy, how's it hangin'?"

Lisa: "Honey!" She slaps his arm. "Be appropriate."

Alex: (audible sigh) "Short, shriveled ... and frustratingly uneventful."

Lisa immediately regrets asking and backs away sloooowly.

Brandon—to Lisa: (he shrugs.) "It's just slang."

Alex: "I mean, … strong, pronged and a bit oblong."

Brandon: "Ya see, Lisa? He's just kidding!"

Alex: "Who's joking? It's all fun and games, 'til someone loses an eye. Brandon! You asked. Ha ha ha!"

Lisa: "Alex, your dancing…" She uses air quotes with her fingers. "Looked pretty intense and energetic. Why the sudden change of pace?"

Alex: Honestly? All of a sudden, it hit me: I'm—regrettably— livin' in the past too much. I'm forty fuckin' three years old! I'm middle aged. Nobody caaares what I did in high school! I've gotta live in the now! Lisa. Got any friends?"

Lisa: (giggles) "Not to worry. From my understanding, smart is the new sexy! Observe. Brandon, when would it be a terrible time to get pregnant and why?"

Brandon: "Well, in 19th century Britain, opium was marketed—for babies—under the name, 'Quietness.' In the singing words of Cher, "If I could turn back tiiiiiome!'"

Lisa: "Jeezus, that is soooo hot!" She leaps up to Brandon and violently makes out with him.

Alex: "Dude, that's great."

Brandon: "What, that we're not in 19th century Britain or that you want my gorgeous wife?"

Alex: "A?"

Brandon: "Is that a question?! Are you asking me? Are you unsure?!"

Alex: (in a stern, no nonsense voice) "Definitely A."

Lisa: "Wow, honey! You were right! I can totally see how funny it is to mess with Alex."

Brandon: "He's sooo focused on his numbers that he just blocks out everything else.

To Lisa: "Watch."

To Alex: "Alex, your suit ripped, and now your ass is hanging out.'"

Zero reaction from Alex.

Brandon: "Jeez! I cannot figure out the only number that has the same amount of letters in its name as its meaning for the life of me!"

Alex instantly snaps his head toward Brandon and yells, "Four!"

Lisa: "Hhhhhmmmmm. Vvveeerrryyy interesting. ... let me try something."

Lisa coyly strides beside Alex, pinches his posterior and whispers in his ear, "I'll never tell."

Alex doesn't so much as blink.

Lisa looks at her slack jawed husband, shows him a peace sign and silently mouths the words, "Phase two."

She decrees: "It's pretty frickin' obvious that the best number is 10,000. I mean, ... it's a hundred hundreds."

Alex snaps out of his (faux) trance.

"Uuum, pardon me, ma'am. But, I beg to differ. Ya see, 73 dwarfs 10,000 not quantitatively but qualitatively. ... the number—73—is the 21st prime number, while its reversal—37—is the 12th. Its binary form—1001001—is palindromic. Two factors of the ten in 10,000 are 5 and 2. The sum of 5 and 2 is 7, and the difference is 3. Ergo, 10,000 makes up the pieces of 73."

Lisa: (semi sarcastically) "Holy cow, Alex! I'm gonna blather to all my friends just how brilliant you are!"

Alex: "... Hhhmmm, that begs the question. Quantity or quality?! I'd rather you just talk me up to only your good friends. ... Rather than to all of your acquaintances."

Lisa: "Ask ... and you shall receive."

FAITH IN NEW PLACES

Seeing as his new friend, Lisa, just volunteered to get the ball rolling with his real-life eHarmony dating process, Alex started to grow more hopeful in the kindness, helpfulness and good graces of others. Ya see, Alex had a rather ignominious past when it came to relying on the good nature of others:

In college, twenty-one plus years ago, Alex had to develop a detailed memory, an indefatigable tenacity, and a me-first motivational attitude. The competitive student atmosphere of Harvard was very much a preview of the hustles and bustles of the real world. From top test grade, to best wrestling record, to most community service hours, these experiences all cultivated Alex's individualism and determination. There were very few team victories during Alex's collegiate career. Hell, there were even fewer teams—in general—at the prestigious university. But Harvard (*Hah vuhd*) constructed Alex's me first psyche and his interminable inner battle to be the best.

There was no one nowadays with whom to compete for romantic bliss. Nevertheless, Alex sought—unashamedly—to better Brandon in terms of romantic relationships. Yes, Brandon was already legally bound to his feminine counterpoint. But, Alex—playfully—saw this detail as a minor, negligible note that could be overlooked. Alex—like an eeeeediot—was setting himself up for failure. How could he beat a fellow angler in a fishing contest, if he lacks appealing bait, and his opponent has already landed a keeper?!

If Alex would look at dating as a fishing expedition, he'd unquestionably feel that size does not matter. Imagining back to his younger days up north, Alex would definitely rather nail a respectable sized walleye or perch, as opposed to a giant eelpout.

Alex shmoozes with Brandon about what each has been up to over the last 25 years.

Brandon: "I've been extremely happy at my job as a marine biologist. I'm studying the different mammalia in each of the four seas surrounding the country of 'Türkiye'—the Sea Of Marmara, the Black Sea, the Aegean Sea and the Mediterranean."

Alex: "Ha ha ha! That reminds me of George Costanza from the hilarious show, *Seinfeld*. 'Member when he said, 'I've always wanted to pretend to be a 'marine biologist.'"

Brandon: (straight faced and unamused) "Well, I don't pretend at all."

Alex: "Ah, yes, bro. I admire that dedication to doing it the right way."

Brandon: "Anything worth doing is worth doing right."

Immediately, Lisa chimes in: "That's what she ... no, that's what I said!"

Alex: "Ha ha ha! *Touché* and amen!"

Brandon: "Speaking of doing it right, I married this goddess on April 8th, 2017. Some eleven years ago."

Alex: (almost immediately clears his throat) "Ah ah ahem! Actually, dude. 'Twas approximately 11.1699 years ago. C'mon, bro! It's simple division. Even your kids would know that."

Brandon: Uuum, we don't have kids yet."

Alex: "Then, hypothetical kids. I don't know about you, Brandon. But, I was defining the *Sieve of Eratosthenes*, when I was merely a twinkle in my father's eye."

Lisa: "Okay. Enough of my smiling and nodding! What the hell is the Sieve of Erat … Eratuhs … That?!"

Alex: (audible chuckle) "The Sieve of Ee-rah-toss-thin-eez is an ancient algorithm for finding all prime numbers up to a given limit."

Lisa: (confused and annoyed) "In English?!"

Alex: "Here, gimme any number."

Lisa: "87, 'Cuz it's my birth year."

Alex: "K. Here we go: 2, 3, 5, 7, 11, 13, 17, 19, 23, 29, 31, 37, 41, 43, 47…"

Brandon: "Grab a chair, hun. Alex will go on to completion. 'Cuz he doesn't mind being an asshole."

Alex smiles sheepishly and continues.

"… 53, 59, 61, 67, 71, 73, 79 and 83. That's 23 primes. Ask, … and you shall receive."

Lisa: "Jeeeezus, Alex! Just for embarrassing my husband, I'll turn your words against you to benefit you! Ask for something! If you're lucky, maybe you'll receive it."

Give a Lil'. Take a Lot

Alex is flattered by Lisa's roundabout offer. However, he is hesitant to reveal his personal wants to a buddy's wife, whom he just met! He debated whether to entrust a newfound associate with his own, private, romantic desires.

Alex thinks: *According to me, she's asexual. Off limits!*

Lisa—to Alex: "Need some time to weigh your options?"

Alex: "Yeah. Do you mind if I take some time to do my homework?"

Brandon, eavesdropping, bursts out laughing: "Ha ha ha … haaa! Wow! You're still a nerd."

Alex: "Yeah, a nerd who can, and did lead you to a football title. And who can, and did, bust your arm, when you kept talkin' shit."

Silence.

Alex: "Game. Set. Match. Kalatovski."

The group has a three-way staring contest of awkward silence.

Lisa: "Leave him alone, honey! Now, the least we can do is find him a partner!"

Alex: "Ha ha ha ha hhhaaaaa!"

Lisa: "What is sssooooo funny?!"

Alex: "I really appreciate your energetic concern, Lisa. But, do you have any idea that your offer of help was completely contradictory?! Was that deliberate? For the irony? Or, have you been eavesdropping on some of your husband's conversations, and some of his witty wordplay rubbed off on you?"

Brandon: "Bro, I'm used to your teasing. But, please! Not my wife."

Alex—to Lisa: "My sincere apologies, Mrs. Whitfield. I was just honoring your marital vows of 'What's mine is yours'."

Alex smiles ... devilishly.

Lisa: (She's secretly sarcastic. Ssssshhhhh!) "I am offended! Did you want my help or not?!"

Aside, out of Brandon's vision, Lisa gives congratulatory daps to Alex and laughs.

Alex: (excitedly but apologetically) "Oh, I do. I do. I duh ooo!"

Lisa: (she motions her head toward Brandon.) "That's what he said! With more 'do's."

Alex—to Brandon: "Really, bro?! Doo doo? At your wedding?!" He quotes Hook: "'Bad form, Mistah Smee!' I hope you had the decency to serve guests a poo poo platter."

Lisa—to Alex: "Sooooo, you want a girl who appreciates smart humor?"

Alex: "And, she doesn't mind a lil' good natured ribbing. She can take a joke if I poke fun at her. I'm fairly big on fun poking."

Lisa: "And inappropriate puns."

Narrow the Search

Brandon excused himself to chat with other football buddies. Lisa remained to talk more with Alex. Lisa claimed to have numerous friends who are smart and funny and …

Alex: "Single! I can only do so many arm locks."

Lisa: "Heeey! Are you implying that your taking down of my husband was a desperate attempt to get me to lower my marital shield?! … 'Cuz that ain't happenin!"

Alex: "Oh, gosh no! It's just a saaad fact that I hafta resort to physical pain to get my point across. I don't want to deem him a 'dumb jock.' But come on! Damnit! I should've mimicked a faux huddle!"

Lisa: "Physical violence on Brandon to get him to do what you want? I know that definitely works! In a totally different way!"

Alex: "T.M.I., Lisa. T. … M. … I."

Lisa: "Hey, if you want me to help you find a potential mate, then you and I are gonna hafta share some personal info."

Alex: "Okaaaaay, fine!" Audible sigh. "But, pleeeeeassse understand that I'd really rather not hear a buddy's private intimate preferences, especially from his wife!"

Lisa: (mocking Alex) "'Okaaaaay.' Fine!" She giggles. I'll try to keep it PG-13. " Lisa snaps to attention. "However! Must I remind you that this is not communist Russia?! Ever heard of the First Amendment? … Of the constitution?!"

Alex: "Actually, yes. It protects the American right to establish and practice a religion, as well as our right to peaceably assemble. Ergo, I'm lookin' to establish a religion of free love and feminine worship. And, I will assemble with the top supporters regularly one at a time." He snickers like a schoolgirl.

Lisa: "Jeeeeez! You really are an annoying brainiac. Oh, and you—ironically—omitted the Freedom of Speech, meaning I am constitutionally entitled to impart information and ideas, regardless of the medium."

Alex: "Touché!"

Lisa: "So, let's continue talking. Note to self: 'Emphasize to ladies that Alex has the ability to hold his own in a lengthy, humorous, intellectual conversation.' They'll find that very attractive! I'm not gonna lie. Females love the sound of their own voices! Sooo, what do you dooo, like professionally?"

Alex: "I'm a film critic."

Lisa: "'Wunderbar!' What an ideal date?!"

Alex: (loud audible sigh) "except that when I'm working, I hafta constantly scribble down notes. So, I'd have little to no time to … be a caring date."

Lisa: "Hhhmmm, valid point. But, that'd be mixing business with pleasure. Can't you go to the movies … for fun and enjoyment?"

Alex: "My 'job' is to have fun and be enjoyable. It's just what I do!"

Lisa: (audible sigh) "You know what I meant."

Alex: "Yeah. I guess I can suck … it … up."

Lisa: (Exasperated sigh) "C'mon! How hard is it to differentiate?"

Alex: "Well, mathematically, differentiating is easy. Socially speaking, *'no comprendo'*."

Lisa: (exasperated sigh) "Jeez. This is gonna be tough! Where's Brandon?"

Good Work Takes Time

Lisa wanders around the auditorium, desperately searching for her husband. Since she attended a different high school some twenty-three years ago, Lisa is unfamiliar with the prevalence of various cults and their divisiveness even twenty-five years later. She frantically examines the attendants for tall, reasonably coordinated athletes—like her husband.

She thought she found the lost city of Atlantis. But, said towering treetops are just the basketball team. Lisa soon begins kicking herself. "Wrong kind of field goal, ya putz!" She chastises herself for not knowing her own husband's sporting lexicon.

After throwin' 'bows (jostling elbows) with a number of tall, lanky, foreign-born beanstalks ("Budheim Tutalovic" was her favorite.), Lisa's frustration very nearly made her throw in the towel. She internally pouted, unaware of her own very visible tears, bloodshot eyes, and protruding lips.

"Awww, what's wrong, babe? Ya gonna squirt some? Ha ha ha." She turned a 180 to stare down menacingly at the cackling, infantile source. She thought: *The guy's probably four foot nothing, with taped glasses.* Instead, she was greeted by a land-living leviathan.

Lisa nervously s st stuh stuttered out: "Uuum. Puh pardon me, Godzilla. But, I can't suh suh seem to fuh fuh find Mr. Buh Brah Brandon Gallegos. Any chuh chah chance you could heh heh help me?"

Leviathan: "Hi. I'm John. John Freedehl. Lucky for you, I do know Brandon from my ol' football days. Unlucky for you, I'd rather be catchin' up with my ol' basketball buddies or wrestling chums than finding all the ex-football players. I remember Brandon and Alex Kalatovski were pretty tight. Maybe he can help you in your search."

Lisa: "I've met Alex, thanks. We're both looking for Brandon. Thanks."

Emotionally exhausted and distraught, Lisa knelt down to—visually—bawl her eyes out. She was careful how she maneuvered her dress slit to avoid exposing her nether region to all.

Thankfully, Alex appeared just then to Lisa's relieved surprise.

Lisa: "How did you find me?! I looked everywhere for you!"

Alex: "When you were fiddling with your dress, I heard it in my heart. I can just hear women's folding their clothes. The crinkling of dress fabric pierces my eardrums like a blue whale's loud, rumbling echolocation. It is possible for me to even guesstimate a woman's distance away, and the volume of friction just from her pants maneuvering. It may be my seventh or, even, my eighth sense. Ya see, I discovered this skill as a young pre-adolescent. I was out on my morning run one Saturday morning, when I heard this woman on the next block grabbing her newspaper. She had been out the night before. She was still wearing her spandex pants. She was kinda heavy set, so I heard the cacophonous friction between her thighs. 'Twas an estimated (he licks his right forefinger then extends it up above his head, as if he's just then detecting the sound through the auditorium's air conditioning.) 188 decibels[10]. Also, I knew she dropped the comics section, 'cuz I heard a giggle. Then, she had a few choice words for Marmaduke the dog. Audible sigh. As if he had any say in his gender determination!"

Lisa: "Seven? Eight senses?!" She giggles. Sounds like neither math

---

[10] That's the loudest blue whale call recorded on a hydrophone.

nor anatomy are your strong suits."

Alex: "Internally, I'm disappointed and crying that you have not yet recognized my mathematical repertoire as almost sickly. But, outwardly, I'm gonna ignore your put down, and just dismiss it as Brandon inspired propaganda. Besides! I consider instant quantification and cinematic quote recall as legitimate—dare I say—enviable senses. Don't hate me because my thought process is beautiful. Go ahead and quote me on that, ... 'cuz chicks dig oddballs, right?! Sooooo, let's get back to work on my soul search, eh?"

Lisa: "K, I'm gonna accentuate that you are terrific at elaborate hyperbole and detailed storytelling."

Alex: "For smart people! That would suck ass if m' lady were to not understand echolocation. Yes. Yes! I do love to entertain with a memorable tale."

TRIAL AND ERROR

Alex enjoyed re meeting old friends and colleagues at the reunion. He was, however, extremely disappointed that he could not attract much feminine interest in his various goings on. He trudges through his own house—alone—the next morning. Alex gobbles up a banana, grabs a handful of strawberries, eats two slices of multi grain toast with peanut butter and raspberry jelly and downs a glass of grapefruit juice. He glances outside to check the weather. Sunny and breezeless.

Alex (quietly aloud to himself): "Hhhmmm. There was Maria. And, Lisa is a forbidden tool … for more future possibilities." He licks his chops, while he surreptitiously rubbing his palms together.

"On that note, I suddenly have the energy for my morning jog."

Alex felt his knees were starting to betray him as he aged. So, he now casually jogged every morning instead of ran. Approximately 42 minutes later, Alex returned home from his jog. He ditched his sweat soaked sweatpants and sweatshirt—an old wrestling habit he never ditched—in about 29 years—to shower.

These activities have become Alex's, almost religious, morning routine:
- light but purposeful breakfast
- while eating, reflect on past day and plan for oncoming day
- ~30+ minute jog around the 'hood

- shower

Since he was busy at his reunion last night, Alex briefly reviewed a few movies in his head, as he drove to work. 'Tis not the most dedication to cinematography, but Alex (how can I say this?) ... knew his shee yite. So, he could afford to cut a few corners with his time management. Besides, now that Alex was—quote un-quote—middle aged, he was all about efficiency. So, he critiqued:

Alex: "I still know what your kid did 30 summers ago." *Audible sigh.* "Kinda entertaining. But, ... same shit, different day. *Boondock Saints III: The Aints.* Wowza!"

Alex arrived at work, got his movie assignments and planned his day.

Alex—to coworker: "Jeez, I feel like I need the movie, *Multiplicity.* There are so many places I need to be and things I need to do at once!"

Coworker: (audible chuckle) "In your case, is there still a 'Rule #1'?[11]"

Alex—to coworker: "FYI. I tend to narrate my life as my decisions play out. So, that last comment was not only not directed at you, but 'twas rhetorical. As my coworker, you should know this! I don't even know your name!"

Coworker: "My name is Peter Simmons, and I've worked here for seventeen months, three weeks, two days and twelve minutes."

Alex: "Great! As a display of respect and an attempt at future socializing, I'm giving you a nickname. It'll be 'Pocket Simon.' Oh, and hats off for your attention to mathematical detail in your employment duration."

Pocket Simon: "Ooo kaaaaay. Might I ask ... why?"

Alex: "Well, obviously, you lack the name calling creativity of a longtime butt of jokes. Lucky you. Now, pay attention 'Simon.' 'Cuz your last name is 'Simmons,' but that's a tad too long. And, 'Pocket', 'cuz... One, your first initial is 'P'."

Simmons: "Wow, 'P' for 'Pocket?' How not creative."

---

[11] Inside joke from the movie, *Multiplicity,* in which the protagonist was adamant about his copies' "not sleeping with [his] wife".

Alex: "But, your initials are also P.S. Much like Pocket Simon. And two, you—newbie—are of little significance to me. So, I consider you changeable or portable."

Simmons: "Portable? So, are you saying that you want me to travel with you?"

Alex: "I plead the fizz ith."

Alex rushed off to his busy day. He saw that he was assigned to review comedic classics. He was ambivalent, 'cuz he enjoyed comedy. But he was hoping to take some notes from some romantic films.

Alex mumbles to himself: "Learning love tips at my work to increase my romantic activity? *Audible sigh.* "I feel like I'm doing this backwards." Alex spent the whole rest of his workday feeling desperately awkward.

Alex—to himself: "Did I accidentally stumble into a classic '81 DeLorean, slam on the gas pedal up to eighty-eight miles per hour[12] and revisit my high school years? 'Cuz this … is … awkward!"

Alex suddenly recalled his attire at work yesterday. "When has an 'F.B.I.' shirt ever been funny? 'Female Body Inspector'? You're better than that!"

---

[12] Reference to the film, *Back to The Future*

Game On

The next evening at her home, Lisa begged Brandon for Alex's phone number. She was so excited that she finally found a few likable friends. She wanted to share the joy.

Brandon: "Ya know, if I were not so trusting of you and our love, then I'd be eerily suspectful of your sudden … obsession with Alex Kalatovski."

Lisa: "Relax, babe! I'm just helpin' the guy out. As I understand, said man was a friend of yours way back when. He complained of his struggles in the romantic realm, complimented our mutual love and greatly desired an affectionate partner. I volunteered to assist in trying to get him back on his feet."

Brandon: "Despite his being a massive nerd, Alex did lead me to a football championship." Brandon (almost silently): Plus, he nearly broke my arm."

Lisa: "Oh, yeeeah! I forgot about his football skills. Wha wha wwwhhhaaaaaaattt?! Broke your arm?!"

Brandon: *Audible sigh.* "The little bastard put me in some kind of weirdo karate armlock. The only way I could escape with two arms was to promise I'd stop being a jerk to wrestlers. I don't wAnna talk about it."

Lisa: "Babe! I'm a nurse! At least lemme inspect it!"

Brandon: "Hun, you're a veterinarian."

Lisa: "And, you're my lion."

Brandon: "Babe, affectionate animalistic metaphors aside. Why would you want to assist that weirdo?"

Lisa earnestly tried to judiciously determine a winner in her ambivalence between her endless love of her husband and her growing respect for and admiration of her new friend. She reluctantly reasoned that friends come and go, but life partners are just that. Teammates for life."

Lisa cautiously stammered: "So, I'm leaning one way. But, show me your arm."

Brandon rolled up his right shirt sleeve to better show his full right arm. As he turned away to better expose his right tricep, he mumbled: "The little shit snuck up on me. He grabbed me from behind, did a bunch of spins, then had me on the ground with my arm locked between his legs."

Lisa countered: "Hhhmmm. Maybe I should take notes." She smiles coyly. Lisa lightly presses on a reddish area on his upper right elbow area. Brandon grimaces.

Brandon: "Ow, ow, ooouuuch! Yeah, there. That's the ticket."

Lisa: "Well, it doesn't look bad. So, the damage must be internal. Let's check your mobility. Here, rotate your arm."

Brandon does so slowly. "No pain there. Would it help your medical analysis, vet, if I acted like an animal?"

Lisa: "Well, hhhmmm. Perhaps, yes." she giggles. "Do a lil' dance in a small circle, and present your buttocks, like a monkey who's doing his mating dance and seeking attention

Brandon: "Strangely, hun, I know exactly what you mean."

As Brandon prances about and protruding his rear, Lisa laughs hard. After several minutes of his goofin', Lisa sought to get down to business. "So, tell me exactly how that little goob hurt my man."

Brandon: "Well, that armlock hyperextended my right elbow sumthin' fierce! I couldn't escape let alone, move!"

Lisa looked concerned, as she hugged Brandon. She laid her husband's head against her chest, as she slowly massaged his upper right arm. But, in Lisa's head, she visualized Alex's dating potential: amazing intelligence, dominating physicality, magnetic personality and charismatic charm.

Husband Love or Friend Help?

Lisa strenuously pondered why she couldn't have both. She had loved Brandon for years. But, she was intrigued at the thought of a new project with a new friend. She had a strong attraction to both people. Just in very different ways. She had zero interest—none—in experiencing Alex's intimate side. But …

Lisa thought: "There has to be a way for me to continue to pamper my hubby, while also playin' matchmaker for my new friend and my old friends!"

Finally! Lisa completed copying a list of all of her friends' phone numbers from her cell phone to an email on her laptop. She also printed the email to give to Alex in person.

After seemingly finishing, Lisa just remembered a vital issue. Alex said he has a terrible fear of flying. So, all the women hafta be somewhat local. She crossed out Lauren in Italy, Carly in California, Leeann in Pennsylvania and Samantha in Washington.

Lisa (to herself): "There. Now I've got a copy online as well as a hardcopy. Textbook preparedness.

After tooting her own horn to no one in particular, Lisa sat down and called everyone on her list to lay the groundwork for Alex's imminent call.

Lisa—to her friend, Teresa: "Hey, girl! What's been going on with you?"

Teresa: "Oh, heeello! I'm alright. How's the married life?"

Lisa: "Just lovely, thanks. How's the single life?"

Teresa: "Rather uneventful, I'm sorry to say."

Lisa: "Those guys don't know what they're missing! May I help you get the word out?"

Teresa: "I don't see why not. It's probably better, or more attractive, if the compliment comes from an outside party—as in not me."

Lisa: "Splendid. I have a groovy, young gentleman who's right up your alley. Smart. Athletic, movie lover. Did I mention he's ridiculously smart?"

Teresa: "He sounds dreamy. When can I meet him?"

Lisa: "Oh, he is! If I weren't married…"

Lisa (to herself but deliberately loudly): "Shut up, Lisa! How 'bout Friday night Teresa?"

Teresa: "Sure, thanks. Wait. Before you give him my number, what's he look like? He's not hideously obese, is he?!"

Lisa: "Not at all! He's about, uuuhm, 6 feet tall, uuuhm, 200 pounds, muscular, blonde hair, blue eyes and one leg."

Teresa: "One leg? Wait. Right or left?"

Lisa: "Which is gone, or which is still there?"

Teresa: "Which is there?! Duh!"

Lisa: "Well, he's not missing his right leg."

Teresa (giggles): "Hhhmmm. I can live with that. Metaphorically speaking. It's way too early for me to declare our living together!"

Lisa: "K. So, Friday night?"

Numero Uno

Friday afternoon came along, and Alex haphazardly drifted amongst his three daily movies for work. He couldn't help but be excited for his imminent date that evening! Thankfully, he pulled classic comedy that morning. So, he already knew his film analyses for his day's selection: *Ghostbusters* (the original), *Dumb and Dumber* and *Groundhog Day*.

Alex—to Simmons: "Just try to see the irony of my critiquing a movie about a single day's unchanging repetition on the same day as my first date in … six years, four months, three weeks and five days."

Simmons: "One. Wow! You actually talked to me! So, I do exist! Ha ha ha. Eat it, therapist.

Two. Actually, I believe it'd be more coincidental than ironic, because irony generally involves two opposite meanings. Like, if you were in a horrific car accident that left you in a coma with a traumatic brain injury, and you failed your airplane piloting test, and your girlfriend dumped you, all on the same day we gave you *Groundhog Day*. A film about constantly repeating the same day over and over … and over."

Alex (slowly inhaling then exhaling): "One. Ya wAnna one up your therapist? Tell him, '*Cogito ergo sum.*' That's Latin for 'I think, therefore I am.' And, he should research René Descartes.

And, two. Ya see? This is why I don't talk to you 'cuz people don't enjoy being corrected all the time. Side comment: way to be uber specific about my bad day. Was that story from a movie?"

Simmons: *Audible sigh.* "Nope. Just the unfortunate story of my cousin. Tragic, really." Simmons sniffles twice. "I don't wAnna talk about it."

Alex: "Hey, you brought it up."

Simmons (very matter of factly): "I was talking to myself."

Alex: "Hey, that way you assure yourself of respecting your audience."

Simmons: "I hate myself."

Alex: "Aaahhh, now I see the necessity of the therapist. P.S. I do not believe in coincidence. Everything has a logical explanation."

Alex pushed through the rest of his workday with relative ease. He was very excited about his date. He used his work connection at a local theater to play a classic for him. Rather than breaking for lunch, Alex nibbled on a bunch of little snacks—like dried apricots and Graham Crackers—throughout the day to maintain his energy. He sought to finish early, so he could go home to finish prepping for the evening. Well, sure enough, he critiqued his three movies for that day, plus he semi wrote up four more for future projects. Thus, Alex exited work forty-five minutes early with a big smile on his face.

After completing his final date-prep routine[13], Alex called the movie theater and the restaurant to make sure all was okay that night. Since everything seemed to be hunky dory, Alex called Teresa to inform her of his imminent departure.

Alex—on phone with Teresa (mimicking the hand gestures of the title character in the 1997 film, *Hercules*): "I am on my waaay. I can go the distance! I know that every mile … will be worth my while."

After hanging up, Alex—to himself: "Gotta leave 'em wanting more!"

Alex drove fifteen minutes to pick up Teresa. He walked up to her

---

[13] Shower, mouthwash, load wallet, make shorts highlight bulge.

front door and rang the bell. After a few minutes, Teresa hurriedly greeted him with a paintball gun.

Teresa: "Alex Kalatovski, I presume?"

Alex: "Teresa Bethstien, I'm hoping?"

Teresa: "You rang. No, literally. You just rang the bell. I am so relieved that you are my date and not those damn kids who've been lightin' poop on fire on my porch! Brat kids and their Spin the Bottle and *Pokémon Go* and hippy music and damn Book of Faces! They're settin' ablaze to what I hope is dog shit just outside my front door! Next time. Next time I tell ya. Bam! Right in the ass! A paintball shot; I mean."

Alex: "Uuummm. … on a lighter note, … how 'bout we go the movies?"

Alex drove the two to the nearby cinema. Teresa wondered about the film time and beverages.

Alex: "Since I don't wAnna be pressed for time, we're gonna see a movie first. Then, we'll go to dinner. … sooo, no popcorn."

Teresa: "Awww, I'm torn! I'm upset, 'cuz I'm hungry. But, I've calmed, 'cuz I understand and appreciate your reasoning."

Alex: "Okay, fine! I'll buy you some Sour Patch Kids. But, you hafta share 'em!"

The two arrive at the theater. They just walk right into the theater sans tickets. Alex greets the girl at the concessions stand with a head nod. She hands him a box of Sour Patch Kids and two large lemonades. He just smiles and silently mouths "Thank You." They casually stroll into auditorium #8, which is completely empty. Teresa picks two seats in the middle aisle of the middle of the rows.

Teresa: "Right … here! This way we're not so close, that we hafta wrench up our necks to see. And, we're not so far, that we miss any minor details."

After the two sat in their chosen seats, Alex clapped his hands three times. The lights faded, and the first preview began.

Teresa: "Okay. How the hell did you do that?! Is this theater like the clapper?" She tries clapping. Just then, the previews switch to the next film.

Alex: "That was just odd timing. Nothing more."

Teresa: "Okay, seriously. How is everything in this theater suited specifically to you?!"

Alex: "Well, I am a film critic by day. So, theaters know me. They've gotta keep me happy for the good of their name. So, I have my … connections."

Teresa: "Nice! So, the staff here are all your bitches?"

Alex: "I don't like to create a faux governing hierarchy, especially with such demeaning titles. But, yes, they set this up for me."

Teresa: "So, they get you whatever you want, and you just write a good theater review?! Wow! Lemme get some popcorn. And a slushie!"

Alex: "Show some self-control, babe. What about dinner?"

The two thoroughly enjoyed the oldie but goodie film, *Caddyshack*. The two debated about whether golf should be considered an actual sport. Alex drove 'em to a lovely restaurant for a romantic dinner. Alex made sure to not order any sausage or beans. He already felt kinda gassy. But, Alex couldn't forget how nonchalant Teresa acted about abusing Alex's occupational control over the theater staff. Therefore, after taking Teresa home after dinner, Alex mentally noted: "Beautiful but too power driven. Currently, the top o' the list, but only by default."

IF, AT FIRST, YOU DON'T SUCCEED, TRY, TRY AGAIN

The next day, Alex met up with Lisa at a local Bennigan's to inform her of his disappointment with his date.

Alex: "Appearance wise, Teresa was …" Alex touches his right thumb, index, and middle finger together, brings them up to his mouth and makes a kissing sound. "Magnifica! But, unfortunately, her personality left much to be desired."

Lisa: "What do you mean? How was she sub-par?!"

Alex: "Well, she seemed overly interested in my occupational privileges and underly enthused about my personal interests."

Lisa: "What do you mean? Didn't she like the movie?"

Alex: "Yes, she did. She did! She was just more concerned with how much I could get away with from the theater staff. I'd rather not exert that much energy convincing her that there's more to me than just movie theatre perks!"

Lisa: "Oh, bummer! Shall we try again?"

Alex: (audible sigh) "Uuum, … hellz yeah! But, please don't mention what I do. As a film critic. I'd rather surprise 'em."

Lisa: "I've already lined up your next lady just in case. Her name is Christina. I'd say she's kinda buxom. She's about 5' 5". She has sandy brown hair with a …"

Alex: "Aaaaand, stop! I'd like to tell myself that I value personality over appearance. Let her surprise me."

Lisa: "That's a damn respectable moral standard.

Lisa giggles.

Lisa: "Personality over appearance. I'm sure that's what Teresa grumbled in her head after she opened the door to … you!"

Alex: (half sarcastically) "Ouch, Lisa. Very ouch. But, ya know what hurts the most? The fact that you beat me to a "that's what she said" joke. Damnit! I'm gettin' old."

Lisa: "Aaawww, don't beat yourself up. As a woman, I would know 'what she said'.

Lisa giggles.

Alex: "Hhhmmm. Touché. So, what did 'she really say'?"

Lisa stares confusedly in awkward silence.

Lisa: "First, she moaned—under her breath, 'cuz she has a thing for well-kept beards. Then she tried to hide her intimate interest by repeatedly groooaning loudly."

Alex: "Wooooow! Where was I for that?!"

Romance in God's House?

In lieu of Alex's malcontent with Teresa, Lisa tried again. She organized a dinner date for that Friday evening with Alex and Christina. Alex drove the more or less twenty minutes to pick her up. As he walked up to her front door, he saw the big wooden cross on the door. He chuckled quietly and lightly shook his head.

When Christina opened the door to greet Alex, he couldn't help but whoop and snort. He could hear the loud liturgical sermon playing on the [house wide] sound system.

Christina: "Are you Alex Kalatovski?"

Alex: "I am. Better questions—if you're not Christina Jones, what the hell are you doing here?! And, why would you open the door. For me?!"

Christina: "Well, by God's good grace, I am Christina Jones. And I chose to greet you, because the Holy Father tells us to open our doors to our neighbors."

Alex struggled to weigh Christina's aesthetic appeal against her personality flaws. But, he dare not outwardly display any disapproval.

"Textbook shitty date," Alex thought to himself. If he voiced his dislike for anything she liked, nothing would go well.

Alex: "You have a very soothing voice, Christina."

Christina: "May we please converse more over dinner?"

Alex: "Wonderful idea! Care for Mediterranean food?"

Christina: "Ooo, exotic! Sure."

Alex: "Great. I know this great Turkish restaurant around here. Well, technically, it's not exactly around here. But, the quality's still there—regardless of location."

Christina grabbed her purse, and the two scampered to Alex's car. Alex started to drive the half an hour to the two's dinner date. They sat in silence for the first ten minutes. Alex broke the lull by asking, "So, Christina, how often do you date?"

Christina: "Well, a more appropriately worded question would be 'How rarely do you date?'"

Alex: "Rare dates, eh? Join the cluh—"

Just then, an inconsiderate driver cut Alex off. So, he braked hard and instinctively shot his right arm across Christina's chest to protect her from whiplash.

Alex: "Dumbass!" Audible sigh. "You alright?"

Christina: "I am. Thanks for preventing my whiplash. My neck is weak. So, thanks!"

Alex chuckled. He'd just done "the move." According to Frank Costanza on ol' school Seinfeld, when a guy slams on the brakes, he reaches to the side to seemingly prevent his female passenger from a violent chest heaving. In actuality, he covertly feels up his companion.

Alex: "So, as I was saying. I am inviting you to join the club of dateless loners. We meet every Monday and Thursday at seven at an abandoned warehouse. And, yes. In choosing our meeting location, the club of dateless loners was trying to ease the mood of the group by humor through irony."

The two finally arrived at their dinner destination. Having eaten at the restaurant before, Alex knew his way around the semi complicated locale. In his peripheral vision, Alex noticed the soccer game on the television at the distant bar. The host greeted him as the two entered.

"'Hoşgeldiniz!'"

"'Hoşbulduk.'" Alex replied.

Christina was fascinated.

"Wow! Was that secret code? How do you know it? Hhhmmm. Wait a tic! Did you tell her to spike my drink?"

Alex (sarcastically): "Yeah. Ssssshhhhh! The coding's about as 'secret' as one's native tongue can be. Ssssshhhhh! Only approximately 81.3 million people know the ... terminology."

Christina: "One, that response was just oozing with sarcasm. I didn't appreciate that. Two, I'm intrigued. What native tongue is that?"

Alex mentally congratulated ... and berated himself. He accomplished his first goal, which was to impress her. Although he took a step back with his unnecessary sarcasm. He talked to her like she was already a close buddy who understood his personality and sense of humor.

"Not yet. Good work takes time," Alex said to himself.

Alex snapped out of his inner diatribe. He implored forgiveness from Christina.

"Pardon me. I was just having an intense conversation with ... one ... two ... three attentive young chaps: Me, Myself, and I. What might you have asked me?"

Christina giggles. "I complimented you on your little back and forth with the hostess, asked what language that was and ..."

Alex: "Thanks. It's Turkish. I studied abroad there. She was gorgeous! Nothing compared to you though!" He chuckles at his own joke. I'm kidding! Sooooo, I know some of the language. The hostess welcomed us in, and I replied with 'we are honored.' ... Aaaaaannnnndddd hhhhhwhat?"

Christina giggles. "Precisely!" She giggles again. "Why are you putting so much emphasis on the 'h'?"

Alex (playing dumb): "Hhhwhatever do you mean?! Are you telling little hhhwhite lies?!"

Christina: "That! Why are you talking like that?"

Alex: "Oh, I'm just trying to amuse myself. I lack focus. I've been told I'm sophomoric. For example, I can't help but occasionally glimpse at the game. The men almost always have a soccer game on during a meal. But, I've gotta set my priorities! I'm dining with a new and gorgeous woman…" The sarcasm kicks in. "Who's maaaaaybe more interesting than the soccer game. Maybe."

Christina giggled again. Christina commented emphatically about how much she was enjoying the relaxed atmosphere and calm aura. Then she mentioned how thirsty she was.

Christina: "Jeez, my throat is parched from my lengthy sermon today. Plus all the laughing you're causing. Yeah, that's right: I'm blamin' you!"

Alex raised his clenched right fist—under the table—in triumph. For being funny.

He smirked. "I'm sorry I'm not sorry. Here, you said you were thirsty? When our waiter comes, say, 'Lütfen bir bardak soğuk su alabilir miyim?'"

Just then, their waiter arrived at their table.

Christina—to the server—about Alex: "What he said."

Before the waiter left, Alex added: "Aslında ikiniz lütfen."

Christina (hesitantly): "Ooookaaaay. What did you just do?"

The waiter quickly returned with their beverages. Alex told him they needed more time to decide food.

Alex: "Reeeee lax! You said you are thirsty. So, I ordered you a glass of cold water. And, I ordered one for myself. Aaand, I told him to roofie yours."

Christina immediately spits out her gulp all over Alex.

Alex dries his face with his handkerchief, composes himself and comments: "Inappropriate time for a joke, eh?"

Christina: "Oh! You were kidding?!"

Alex: "Note to self. Imaginary roofies are not funny."

Christina: "Sooo, what's good here?"

Alex: "Well, it depends on what you like. Personally, I'd recommend the iskender kebab. You're not a vegetarian, are you?"

Christina reads the dish description. "Delightful. I think I'll try it."

Alex closes his menu to resume their back n' forth.

"As for appeteasers, what do ya like?"

Christina: "Well, weird as it may seem, I've always been partial to chickpeas."

Alex: "Weird. Craving for chickpeas?! That wouldn't even be strange if you were pregnant. To each, her own."

Christina: "Pregnant?" She giggles. "I think pretty highly of myself. But, I cannot have an immaculate conception!" She giggles again.

Alex looks confused.

Christina clarifies. "Well, one, I'm a children's pastor at the Missions of Jesus Followers Church just outside of Pembroke Pines. Hence the theological reference. Two, I do not go out much. At all." She shrugs. "'Cuz I'm so involved with my work? And, three I kinda only see kids all day. So, I'm not gettin' pregnant! ... unless, ... it's by god's good grace."

Alex: "I am honored that you took a..." He does air quotes with his fingers. "Break from..." He does air quotes with his fingers. "Your kids to..." He does air quotes with his fingers. "Go out for this..." He does air quotes with his fingers. "Non work with me!" He mimics wiping sweat from his brow. Their waiter returns for their food orders. Alex orders appetizers for the both of them plus a little extra.

ROMANTIC APPETEASERS ASIDE

Christina remarks how impressed she is with Alex's comfort with all the foreign culture.

"Wow, you really know your way around this culture—the language, the food, the customs. She raises her voice. A popular player scored in the game. "What is it—Greek?"

Christina had forgotten that Alex already stated that the restaurant was Turkish. At the mention of the neighboring people, a hush came over the crowd between mumbled grumbling and muttered expletives.

Alex quickly stood and yelled to the entire restaurant: "Reeelax, everyone! She's just so committed to her job that she doesn't watch the news. She just assumed that all the trouble making and stupid tomfoolery was done by a Greek. Ha ha ha. Go figure, right?"

The crowd—collectively—yells, "Oooooh!" They all followed that with an audible sigh of relief.

Christina—to Alex: "Jeez. Sorry."

Alex: "A word to the wise. The Turks and the Greeks hate each other. A lot! So, try to not confuse the two. Especially aloud.

Christina: "Aaaaahhhhh. Good to know! Thanks a lot!"

Alex: "Still thirsty? Order an 'Ayran'. There's no alcohol."

Alex waves to get their waiter's attention. He said, "Lütfen'", and waved his hand, keying Christina to speak.

Christina—to their server: "One 'Ayran', ... please."

Alex grabs the server: "'Aslında ikisi lütfen.'"

Christina: "I am very apprehensive about your knowing the language and my not."

Alex chuckles, as he extends his right arm so, his hand is really in Christina's face.

"Don't you 'trust me, 'Rose'?."

Christina giggles. "This isn't. What movie was that? *Titanic!* Are you implying that we're bound for a tragic downfall?"

Alex compliments her quick wit. "Touché, … Rose! Naw, I was referencing the film, merely 'cuz of the 'trust' quote. Would you rather I had quoted *Pocahontas*?"

Christina giggles. "No, actually. I am unfamiliar with the cartoon."

Alex: "Au contraire. The fact that you knew 'tis an animated film contradicts your claim of cinematic blindness. Besides! Characterizing you—a brown haired female—as John Smith—a blond haired male—is a bit unbecoming."

Christina: "Gosh darnit! Your vocal analysis saw right through my cinematic facade! Okay, Alex. Let's test your film trivia knowledge. Which character—in any movie—do I most closely resemble?"

Their server returns with two glasses of 'Ayran.' He takes their food orders—from Alex. One iskender kebab and one köfte.

Alex: "Okay. Please disregard my earlier comments about the Titanic, when I cheers to you and say, 'Bottoms Up!'"

Christina giggles. "Oh, sweet irony! Not funny."

Christina: "Ooo, wow! Kinda tastes like Greek yogurt."

Alex: "Sssssshhhhh! Did you already forget the Turk Greek feud about cultural creations? My gut is telling me that these Turkish food connoisseurs are not very understanding!"

Christina: "Oooh, shoot! Should I yell my apology?!"

Alex: "In addition to your apology, scream this food for thought: 'The word, yogurt, actually originally comes from the Turkish word, yoğurt, pronounced yoh urt.'"

Know Your Surroundings

Christina boldly stood up and yelled her apology and word derivation explanation. Afterwards, she said—in a quiet aside—to Alex: "Hey, I just got that pun: yoh urt is food for thought! Very clever!"

The server brings their food—one iskender kebab and one köfte. Each diner—Alex and Christina—eyed the other's meal wantingly.

Christina: "Your food looks delicious! I've always loved a good cheeseburger.

Alex: "Yes! I figured as much. That's why I ordered this simple mock hamburger: to share it with you."

Christina: "Um, I'll try it. But, I should've mentioned that I'm a very picky eater. So, all these tomatoes and peppers and onions kinda freak me out. While your burger looks delicious!"

Alex: "If I learned anything way back in kindergarten, it's sharing time is happy time. Sooooo, what's mine is yours."

Christina: "What's mine is yours? Are we getting married?!"

Alex: "Married? Already?! I know I'm pretty." He tosses back his hair and hikes up his imaginary skirt to show a little leg. "But, ease up on the love train! I mean, we're just talking about sharing food. On our first date! Anyway, let's eat … each other's dinner."

Christina giggled yet again. She pushed her plate toward Alex and pulled Alex's plate toward herself.

"Pardon me," she begged, as she voraciously forked a large mouthful of Alex's köfte into her mouth.

Alex sarcastically: "Jeez! Eat much? May I please feed you? I kinda know the good food combinations and amounts. Plus, it'd be kinda kinky!"

Christina: "I wouldn't know 'kinky' if it snuck up behind me and slowly kissed my neck, as it massaged my shoulders and caressed my inner thighs."

Alex: "Note to self. Massages are kinky."

TRY SOMETHING NEW

After the two finished the eating portion of their own and each other's meals, Alex decided to continue his attempt to impress. When their waiter came to clear the plates, Alex quietly inquired of him:

"'Lütfen, bir şişe rakı, iki bardak ve biraz su içebilir miyiz?'"

After the waiter left with their dirty plates, Christina suspicious, interrogated Alex.

"What'd you say now? Is he gonna sew my eyes shut with wire? Did he put something in my food?"

Alex: "Chill, Christina! One. I merely asked, 'May we please have a bottle of rakı, two glasses and some water?' in Turkish. Two, why would anyone sew your eyes shut?! And three, um, we shared food. So, anything bad in your food I'd have eaten too. Duh!"

Christina: "Um. Yeah. ... That's right! We did share food! Quick! What's ... nine hundred and eighty seven, times ... three hundred and twenty-one?"

Alex: "Hhhmmm."

Christina: "Yep, you're drunk. I'm calling Uber."

Alex: "First of all, how could I be drunk? We both only drank water. Secondly, it's three hundred and sixteen thousand, eight hundred and twenty-seven. Yeah, that's correct ... from a drunkard."

Christina: "Seriously? Wow, you are like a calculator!"

The waiter returns with the requested goods. Christina was very impressed by Alex's math. Now, she's confused as to the new liquid.

Christina: "More water?! Wow, you read my mind, that I'm still thirsty!"

Alex exclaims to Christina: "How delightful! Now, this'll be a fun experiment."

Christina: "Experiment? Whatever do you mean? I am quite sure about and comfortable with my… She lowers her voice to a hush. "Limited, … heterosexuality."

Alex: "Reeeeelax! 'Tis not that kind of 'experimenting'! I'm talking about science. Specifically, chemistry. And, maaaybe a lil' fluid dynamics. I am not speaking in slang. P.S. As a math fan, I love to manipulate limits."

Christina gives a big, semi-seductive smile. "Hey, propz to me for just recognizing the possible slang term! I'm not just a teacher. I actually listen to what the kids say!"

Alex chuckles. "Way to go, Christina, on seeing the potential slang that was not even my intention! Hhhmmm. What are the kids saying these days?"

Christina: "What's rakı?"

Alex: "Really? That's what the word on the street is?! The street thugs are hustlin' rakı?!"

Christina semi jokingly: "Well, they would, … if you said what it is!"

Alex: "Well, in layman's terms, rakı is the unsweetened, alcoholic national drink of Turkey. It smells and tastes like licorice. But, warning…"

Christina giggles. "Whoa, whoa, … whoa! Are you giving me a butt warning?!"

Alex chuckles. "As I was saying. Warning! Rakı is a 90 proof. That's a 45% alcohol by volume. So, it'll get ya drunk! However, on a more comforting note, rakı is often referred to as aslan sütü, or lion's milk, 'cuz it's widely considered the 'milk of the strong'."

Christina: "So, it tastes like licorice, and it's like a strengthening milk? Where do I sign up? Gimme both glasses!"

Christina lunges for the liquor. But, Alex snatches it away.

NEW (NOT ALWAYS) = GOOD

Alex was torn. He was excited Christina was so gung ho about the rakı, which—in turn—aroused the amygdala of his brain. Buuuuuut, Christina was small and likely not used to imbibing much alcohol. Thus, he was wary of her eagerness to cut loose. Turkish style.

He explained his pushing away of the drink.

"Need I repeat that rakı is approximately 9/20 alcohol? Thus, your petite-ness indicates that you have less body water than a larger person, say … me. Plus—and this is not chauvinistic, your femininity combined with heavy alcohol intake hints at an increased likelihood of liver disease, brain damage and breast cancer. It's just science."

Christina: "But, I'm a health nut! I think I …"

Alex: "Eehh! Any argument is moot, 'cuz … it's science."

Christina: "Well, my faith upends your so-called scientific infallibility. So, lemme try this stuff!"

Alex internally battled his own dismay at her religious stubbornness. He dared not show how upset he was. He audibly sighed.

"Agree to disagree."

He fills each glass a third of the way with rakı. So, each could take a shot.

Alex: "Okay. First, we'll take a shot … straight up."

Just as Alex was raising the glass to his mouth, Christina grabbed his hand.

Christina: "Nooooo! You're driving! Me. So, that's precious cargo!"

Alex: "Aah! Good call. I was just tryin' to be polite. To give you a drinkin' buddy. Nobody likes to drink alone."

Christina very matter of factly: "Um, maybe that's true in your heathen neck o' the woods. But, in God's house, we care for others."

Alex: "Fine. Aaaaand, down the hatch!"

He makes a motion of raising an imaginary shot glass to his mouth, overturning it, then rubbing his belly in enjoyment. Christina lifts the glass to her lips, tilts her head back, and overturns the glass. She closes her eyes, shakes her head, and licks her lips in pleasurable satisfaction."

"Whoa! Definite licorice taste."

Alex—concerned—asks: "Is that good or bad?"

Christina: "On Easter Sunday, I trade all my jellybeans for the kids' Twizzlers."

Alex asks hopefully: "Nice. Savin' any Hershey's kisses for me?"

Christina leans in and plants a big wet one on his cheek.

Alex reacts cheerfully: "Score!"

Alex readies the rakı again.

"Now, we have phase 2."

Christina: "Phase 2'?! There's more?! I'm still ... trying to recover from phase 1!"

Alex: "Obseeerve and cherish."

Alex pours about a shot's amount of rakı in Christina's glass. He grabs the glass of water. He starts slooowly pouring the water into the partially filled glass of rakı. Strangely, the rakı changes color from clear to a milky white.

"Aaah, science," he gushes.

Christina blurts out: "What is happening? And, how?"

Alex: "Oh, lovely! So, I'm impressing you."

Christina: "I shan't lie, babe. You haven't stopped impressing me all night!"

Alex turns aside and pumps his fist with a quiet "yeeeees!"

Alex: "Ya see, rakı is a heavily anisette liquor that uses terpenes in its flavoring."

Christina: "Slooooow down! What is 'Anisette'?! … and, what are 'terpenes'?

Alex: "Class is in session! Anisette is a liquor flavored by aniseed. And, 'cuz I know you'll ask, aniseed is the aromatic seed of the anise plant, and it is what gives rakı its licorice like taste and smell. Terpenes are insect repellents that are also highly odiferous. So, the combination of the two makes the licorice flavor strong."

Christina downs another shot. She begs Alex for another.

Christina: "May I pleeassse have one. No, two more shots of the stuff?! It's sssooooo good!"

Alex: "Alright, you forced me into this. We're playin' our first role playing game. Yay! You brought this on yourself."

Christina rolls her eyes and eagerly awaits more rakı.

Alex: "I'm gonna play the role of responsible adult. And, you're obviously playing the role of sophomoric child who's old enough to drink. Anyway, I forbid you from drinkin' more tonight."

The two kiss and pack up to depart. As a joking test of her sobriety, Alex tells Christina to calculate the bill. Christina glances over the numbers and dry heaves!

"Math makes me." She dry heaves. "Uuuggghhh! I couldn't do this, even if I were sober and had a calculator!"

Alex raises his index finger to his chin—in heavy thought, looks through the menu for their food prices and gives Christina exactly x dollars and y cents to go pay the bill.

Alex thinks—to himself: "My, how inflation has devastated our economy!" He left 21.67% of the amount he gave Christina on the table as gratuity. Christina presents the bill and the money to the cashier. After punching in all the prices on the cash register, the cashier accepts Christina's money and hands her back one cent as change. At first, Christina freezes with astonishment.

Christina—dumbfounded—thinks: "How did Alex—a man—determine our entire meal cost in less time it took the register—a machine?" She walks the bill change back to Alex, who was out at the car.

"Penny for your thoughts?" She flips the penny over to Alex with her thumb. "How did you just do that? You just calculated our entire bill in your head in less time it took the cash register an actual machine!"

Alex shrugs his shoulders. "I don't know. I just see numbers everywhere. It's kind of a blessing and a curse."

Christina looks quizzical. "A curse? How so?"

Alex responds: "Say we're out at an art museum. You are marveling at the beautiful paintings.

But, my mind can't help but try to calculate the number of brushstrokes the artist used in each designated section!"

Christina shakes her head. "Oh, jeez!"

Alex drives her home. They exchange phone numbers, kiss good night and part ways. But first, Alex makes sure Christina gets in safely and is situated, 'cuz she is ... wasted!

So Far, So Good

Alex makes sure to call Lisa the next day—Saturday—to tell her how his date went.

Alex—to Lisa via cell phone: "Top notch! It was, like, wowza!"

Lisa: "That's what she said!"

Alex: "Actually, that's literally how she rated it. She liked the restaurant. She liked the food. She loved the rakı! She liked my math. She loved my jokes!"

Lisa: "So, Cupid's arrow struck true. How lovely!"

Alex: "For the most part, yes. However, I just don't like how obsessed she is with religion and beliefs, as opposed to science and facts. 'Tis not my cup o' tea. But I think—I hope—I can look past that for the overall good."

Lisa proudly exclaims: "So, my work here is done!" She pats herself on the back.

Alex retorts: "Actually. I was thinkin' … that I should … try a few more dates, … with different women. Just to better determine if Christina's a keeper. Does that type of thinking make me a bad man?"

Lisa: "Weeell, to a woman, yes. That ain't cool. Females don't like to be judged like animals in a beauty show. But, to not be completely biased, let's get a man's opinion."

Alex: "Hey, I'm a man. Don't my thoughts matter?"

Lisa makes a disgusted face, as if to say, "Eeeeeewww, not for me!"

Lisa yells an aside: "Brandon, honey! Please come give us a man's thoughts."

Alex burns an imaginary hole in his bedroom wall with his fiery, wide eyed glare, as he imagines Lisa's ignoring him. If looks could kill.

Lisa—to Alex—over phone: "I've gotta consult with my hubby. I'll call you back in ten. Bye."

She hangs up.

Brandon emerges. "Wassup, babe?"

Lisa: "I was just on the phone with Alex. He set up a bit of a predicament. I gave my thoughts. But now we need a man's point of view."

Brandon: "Uuuuummm, and what might Alex be?"

Lisa: "Hun, I've recently found that Alex's very fun to mess with? What, do you—of all people—object to my considering him less than a man? Anyway, despite a mostly successful date, he still wants to date other women. If he was so happy with her, why try others? I'm confused."

Brandon: "Chill, darling. He's just thinkin' long term. He's just investigating all applicants, before he selects his winner. That's what I did with you. If anything, at his age—that's good that Alex's Thinkin' long term. He's all about commitment. But, he's thinkin' he's gotta sow his wild oats in a trial by error sorta way."

Lisa: "Whoa, whoa, … whoa, Brandon! It's metaphor overload! You're confusing me."

Brandon: "I apologize, hun. Should I speak sssllloooooohhherrr?"

Lisa gasps. "You'd better speak slowly now, 'cuz your talkin' will be fast and high pitched with my foot up your bottom!"

Brandon: "Ouch, hun! You're usin' my own words against me? Ouch. And, for future reference, hun, it's aaaasssssss, not bottom."

Lisa: "K, sweetie. I've gotta call Alex back. So, you support his wanting other girls? I can't say I support or even understand that."

TRIAL BY FIRE

Lisa reluctantly calls Alex back. She had debated whether she should set him up only with bad friends of hers, just so they'd make Christina seem better by comparison. After an intense inner psychological back n' forth, Lisa's respect for her husband's opinion wins out over her loyalty to her friend. Plus, Alex seems like a good guy. So, she'll try more girls.

Lisa—on the phone with Alex: "Hey, there. So, tell me what you want." Audible sigh. "Now."

Alex: "So, I take it Brandon supported me legitimately? He always was a reliable teammate."

Lisa: "I still don't agree with you. But, it's one on two. I'm fightin' a losing battle. Sooo when are you lookin' to see contestant number two?"

Alex: "Well, since I'm not getting any younger, I'm thinkin' the sooner the better. How 'bout next Friday?"

Lisa: "Okay. I've got the woman. I'll just tell her. Alex Kalatovski will pick you up at about 5:30 Friday afternoon for dinner and a movie. K?"

Alex: "Negative. Make that 'movie then dinner.' That way we can't be late for the film, … 'cuz of our eating."

Lisa: "Good call, Alex. Textbook time management. I'll call you tomorrow. Byyyye!"

Lisa calls Anna Reeves—a driving instructor for the department of motor vehicles. She was pencil thin and stood only about 5'5". Lisa had her reservations, 'cuz Anna was only thirty-one.

Lisa tried to cater to her audience by altering the tone of her speech to the young'un.

Lisa—to Anna: "Hey, grrruuuuurrrl! So, you psyched for your date?"

Anna: "Hellz yeah, I am! What's he like?"

Lisa: "He's Alex Kalatovski. He's about six feet tall, about two hundred pounds, with blond hair, blue eyes and no, he's not a Nazi. He's forty-three years old. He's very experienced in martial arts. And, he's a film critic."

Anna: "Wow, noice! But, would you mind not tellin' him what I do?!"

Lisa: "Uuum, sure. Why not?"

Anna: "It'll just be another discussion topic."

Lisa—visibly confused: "Ooooohhh kkkaaaaay."

Lisa hushed and under her breath: "Yeah, riiiight! If you're extremely lucky, it will."

Anna semi heard her: "What was that?"

Lisa calls upon the limited, sophomoric slang she's picked up from eavesdropping on her church kids' conversations: "In a guy's siiiight, he'll think you're really sucky, still."

Anna frowns. "So, what would you suggest?"

Lisa: "Now, I would tell you to just smile and nod at most everything he says, 'cuz most guys like the sounds of their own voices. But, Alex's not 'most guys.' He seems genuinely interested and authentically concerned."

Anna: "Wow! Nice! Are you sure he's not better than your husband?!"

Lisa: "Uuuuummm. I plead the fifth." Ear to ear smile.

Lisa: "Kidding aside. Alex says he'll pick you up for dinner and a movie, ... Excuse me. Movie then dinner at about 4:30 pm next Friday evening."

Anna: "Next Friday? So, do you mean, in six days or in thirteen days? Your vagueness is killin' me! We're talkin' about my life!"

Lisa: "Jeez, Anna! You're comin' at me too hot. Take a chill pill. Seein' as—according to the Gregorian calendar—the week officially begins on a Sunday, and today's Saturday, next Friday would have to indicate in six days. Would it not?"

Anna as if she has her foot in her mouth: "Oh. Yes, I suppose so."

GOOD SCORE? BAD SCORE?

Alex drives to pick up Anna for their date. Thankfully, she lives close by. Alex adds a point in her favor on his mental scoring sheet. After he parks in her driveway, Alex checks his watch. "4:28? Well done, broheim!"

As Alex strolls up to the front door, he can't help but notice all the pictures of well-kept women adorned with sparkling jewels. He wonders: "Materialistic?"

Anna throws open the door just as Alex reaches for the doorbell.

"Hi, Alex! Wow! I've gotta thank Lisa, 'cuz you…" Anna looks him over from his head down to his feet. "Niiiiice!"

Anna steps outside and leans to shut the door. Alex looks confused.

"Who is this 'Alex' you speak of? And, please don't shut your door. I'm gonna rob you."

Anna's heart sinks. Her heart skips two beats.

Alex: "Naw, I'm just kidding. What dumbass robber would actually say 'I'm gonna rob you now,'? But, I really had you goin', didn't I? I take it, you're Anna?" He peers inside the house. Oh, my! You have a lovely home! … Not to rob. Chillax. To admire."

Anna: "Damn you, Alex! Now I've gotta go change, 'cuz your lying so terrified me, that I peed a little. So, rather than sit in damp panties, I hafta put on new ones. You brought this on yourself."

Alex: "Mind if I just step inside, while you take care of …" He sticks out his hand and shakes it. "What not?"

Anna: "No problem! Come on in. I'll just be a minute."

The two step inside. Alex admires the jewelry and pictures. Only women in jewelry ... Everywhere. As he bends down to admire some jewels on some classic, brass faced, watering cans, he yells, "These are some really nice cans you've got here. Are they European designed?"

Just then, Anna appears right beside Alex. So, as he tilts his head up, he sees that he was face to face—so to speak—with Anna's bosomy chest.

Anna replies, "Surprisingly, no. Many have asked if they're Western European—specifically, Swedish. But, they're just from ol' fashioned Oregon."

Alex: "Ha ha ha! Way to catch the unintended double entendre! I meant these watering cans. But you seem gung ho about talkin' about your chest. I'm not gonna stop you! To the car!"

Alex hurries the quick drive to the theater. By instinct, Anna's occupation takes over, and she becomes a backseat driver. From the passenger seat. Up front.

Anna criticizes Alex's inconsistent turn signaling, his turn speeds, even his hand placement on the steering wheel.

Alex desperately defended himself. "I'm just very comfortable with the route to this theater."

Anna really liked how Alex arranged for a private showing of the classic comedy, *Dumb And Dumber*. The only part she didn't like was when Alex forbade her from ordering a 'Large' popcorn. After the film, the two scooted off to a nearby restaurant for dinner.

Alex: "I always aim to spoil, because that's just what I do. I've got a lot. So, why not share?!"

As they pull up to the restaurant, the concept finally clicked for Anna. "Ooooohhh! By not buying me popcorn, you were ensuring I wouldn't 'spoil' my appetite. But, didn't you just say that you 'always aim to spoil'?"

After hesitating, Alex finally acknowledges Anna's question. "Ha ha ha! Well, in a way, yes, I did say that. But, …"

Anna: "… Not in a literal way! Ha ha!"

Alex: "Aaahhh, it's great that we're both so comfortable with each other's humor. Ice breaker. Check!"

The couple stroll into the Oriental restaurant. The host immediately seats them and fetches their waiter. Alex doesn't mention his extensive martial arts background, which provides him knowledge of the oriental language, customs and food. He prefers to pleasantly surprise her. He's eaten here before.

Anna: "Uuummm. I'm a virgin."

Alex: "Ex squeeeze me?"

Anna: "Sushi virgin. I'm from Oregon. There just aren't that many sushi roamin' around the 'Beaver State'."

Alex handles the food, ordering and further impressing Anna with all his Japanese speaking. The two thoroughly enjoy Alex's selections, even the *amazake* saki. Anna sought to not become a stumbling drunkard. She only has one glass. An admitted lightweight, Anna feels a bit woozy nonetheless.

Anna: "Well, that was an okay meal. I think I've all I can stomach. Shall we?" She motions toward the door.

Alex frowns. "I'm sorry you didn't better enjoy the great food. The company was … slightly better."

Anna: "Only 'slightly'?"

Alex: "Jeez! Must I spell out the true meanings of my sarcasm?" Alex sighs audibly. Kay. Here goes: I space r-e-a-l-l-y space l-i-k-e space y-o-u. Period. No! Exclamation point."

Anna smiles coyly, as the two walk to the car, after Alex pays the bill.

Does the End Justify the Means?

Anna wantingly stares at Alex throughout his entire drive to her house. Upon arriving at her home, Alex politely walks her to her door.

Alex: "Sooo, I'd rate that as a very pleasant evening! May I please sco' yo' digits?!"

Anna: "Ha ha haaa! Your trying to speak like a young ruffian is pretty hilarious!"

Alex: "I hope that you're laughing with me and not at me! And, your phone number?"

Anna: "Why you in such a hurry?" She unlocks her front door, shuffles inside and motions for Alex to follow. Alex excitedly plays the cliché making-love "bow wow chickuh bow wow" song in his head. But, his conscience kicks in at the last minute.

Alex's inner voice: "Gotta give her one last chance to pull out. Jeez, Alex! 'Pull out'? Can't you, at least, imagine better diction?!"

Alex's outer voice—to Anna: "okay. You're in safely, and you're still semi coordinated. Ha ha. Nice night. Well, see ya."

Anna: "Nooooo, please stay!"

Alex plays dumb. "Why? I completed my responsibilities. I provided visual entertainment, nourishment, and interesting conversation. My work here is done."

Anna reemerges from her bedroom. She's changed outta the heels and discarded her top. So, she greets in just her brassiere and skirt.

Alex—clearly upset with himself, because of her minimalist outfit: "Well, damnit!" Alex sighs, exasperated. "But, I've got alotta work to catch up on. I can stay… But only 'cuz I downloaded my work onto my phone. But, I've got class early in the morning. So, I've gotta head out early."

As it turns out, Anna misses an energetic punctuation to mark the end of the date. She falls right asleep seconds after Alex settles beside her. Understanding how self-conscious and self-deprecating women can get postdate, Alex decided to not just let himself out. Plus, that *Saki* must have done a number on her. Alex sighs, chuckles, and mumbles quietly, "Extreme lightweight."

He leans over to kiss her forehead, unlocks his phone, and stays the night.

Inner Questioning

Alex remains awake almost all night. He isn't uncomfortable with the new surroundings. Alex is not very picky about his sleeping location. He is just not physically able to sleep with so many unresolved psychological issues rumbling in his head.

Why did she immediately fall asleep without making love? With her extreme beauty, she can't be used to such disappointment. That's what guys do. Therefore, am I the bitch now? So, who wears the pants?!

Will she think less of me, 'cuz I didn't put out on the first date?

Alex looks around the bedroom.

Why are her guests' condoms in a dish on the dresser? In plain view?!

Why does she have so many condoms? … in different sizes?

Was my conversation that bad that I put her to sleep?

I didn't brush my teeth before bed. So, what if my breath reeks, when I kiss her in the morning? Plus, she didn't like the sushi!

Does she have mouthwash?

How's her bathroom look?

Will she get offended, if I do not call her for future dates?

Shitballz! What's her phone number?

Shitballz! I forget her job!

What if she works on Saturdays?

So, that's why she has so many jewelry pictures. She's a big bedazzling fan! What are the kids calling it these days—vajazzling?

Did she hafta critique my driving so often?
How long will she continue that?
Is it absolutely necessary?!
Can I tolerate it?
... for how long?
Am I a bad guy for even possibly contemplating weighing my sexual happiness over her psychological discourtesy?
What if she wants a second date?
If so, when can I allow a friendly date ... between acquaintances?
Tomorrow?
Too soon?"

Too Much of a Bad Thing?

At about 5:30 in the morning, Alex finally falls asleep. So, he is understandably exhausted, when Anna exits her bed at around 8:00 am. After urinating, Anna returned to snuggle with Alex. She initiated some playful conversation: "Well, that sleep was absolutely wonderful!"

Alex was visibly confounded: "A little clarification please? As to why you think 'twas so enjoyable? Are you referring to the movie, the conversations, the attempted late night sexcapade or the sleeping company? I know you're not referring to the sushi!"

Anna retorts: "Um, all of the above. Minus the sushi. How do you know so much Japanese? Are you a spy? Don't lie…" Anna makes air quotes. "…for your country!" She continues, "Hhhmmm. What can you tell me, that you know, about 'Fat Man' and 'Little Boy'[14]?"

Internally, she thought: *You are incredibly thoughtful for spending the night here with me! I shouldn't tell you that I want more. That'd just seem … too needy. … Aaawww, what the hell?*

Anna purposefully marches to her bed, hops aboard, and straddles a supine Alex.

Anna—aloud: "How 'bout trial two? Am I hotter in the morning?"

Alex shakes his head disappointed: "Class."

---

[14] These were the code names of the two atomic bombs dropped by the United States on the Japanese cities of Nagasaki and Hiroshima, respectively.

Anna: "Aaawww, fuck no!'"

Alex: "Um, previous commitments call. But I like your enthusiasm. You get a gold star."

Anna: (sarcastically) "Oh, yay! My mom will be so proud."

Alex frowned and sighed. "If you're tryin' to be romantic, and sweep me off my feet, then ... could you be more awkward?! Way to kill the moment, Anna, by talkin' about your mom and makin' me feel real old!"

Anna apologized sincerely. "My bad, bro!"

Alex is really getting frustrated: "Enough with the slang! Are we brozephs on the streets? 'Cuz you are tryin' to be freaks in the sheets!"

The two settled down and eliminated all non-romantic talk. Was great ... for about 15 minutes. Then, Alex couldn't resist.

"Since you've already mentioned your mom, please don't call me your daddy! I don't know what you're into. But, as a man with four brothers, ... incest just does not get my juices flowing. And, do not ask me if I'd rather be your sibling or your parent. 'Cuz either one would make my penis dwarf back into my lower abdomen. As an innie. Boooo urns!'"

Anna emits a loud, boisterous laugh. "Were you saying, 'boooo' or 'boo urns'?"

Alex: "I was saying boo urns.'"

He chuckles. "Nice. You get the *Simpsons* reference. Now, no more laughing at me. I've gotta go."

As Alex gets up to leave, Anna states: "Well, hopefully, you'll eventually be more my 'daddy' than my 'brutha'."

Alex fakes a halfhearted smile. He drives home. While driving, however, Alex makes the horrible realization that he still is clueless as to Anna's phone number.

He yells at himself: "Sonuvabitch!"

After actually pondering swinging a you ee to drive back, Alex assuages his own panic and worry by closing his eyes at the next stoplight, inhaling deeply, and exhaling audibly. He repeats this process three times, before the light turns green.

"Oh, well. If it's meant to be, it'll find a way to be."

Despite the excellent chemistry and joke references there, Alex just cannot get over their conversational dichotomy on many issues: timing and propensity of slang usage, incestual turn ons and driving etiquette. Alex is relieved to conclude that conceptual harmony beat physical bliss in this instance.

Yay! I am not a whore, since there was no sex involved. Wait, does whore imply a woman? Okay, I'm a mhore—a man whore. But, that sounds like Moor, and I am not a 15th century Arab Muslim in Northern Africa. Don't whores get paid? I bought everything last night. W.T.F.?

SQUARE IN THE CIRCLE HOLE

The next day—Sunday—Alex reports back to Lisa, that he really likes some parts of Anna. But he doesn't agree with the whole.

Lisa—on phone with Alex: "New contestant? When?"

Alex: "How 'bout this Tuesday evening for 'movie and dinner'?"

Lisa: "'Movie and dinner' again? Jeez, you really like that set up."

Alex: "Hey, if it ain't broke, don't fix it. Right?"

Lisa: "Well. It could always be better. Right? Okay. I've tentatively got a lady lined up for you. I'll call you later to confirm."

Lisa hangs up on Alex to call her friend, Marguerita. Marguerita Fernandez is a Spanish teacher at the same high school where Lisa works teaching Language Arts. The two originally befriended each otheryears ago, as each was frustratingly critiquing her own native tongue in the teachers' lounge. Marguerita stands about 5' 7" and is of a medium build.

Lisa—into her house phone: "Hello? Marguerita?"

Marguerita: "Um, Lisa?"

Lisa: "Indeed, it is. Marguerita?"

Marguerita: "¡Hola, mi amiga! ¿Cuál es la buena palabra?"

Lisa: "C'mon, girl! You know I don't speak such a simple language. How 'bout a date with a classmate of my husband's?"

Marguerita giggles.

Marguerita: "I merely asked you, 'What's the good word?' and, that is a 'good word'! When would I meet him?"

Lisa: "How 'bout this Tuesday evening? For dinner and a movie? Excuuuse me—movie then dinner."

Marguerita: "Ah, que bueno. Early movie leads to late night!"

An awkward look crosses Lisa's face. "Oooooookaaaaay." She just smiles and nods.

Lisa calls Alex to confirm his Tuesday date at the local movie theater at 4:30 with dinner reservations for 7:00.

Alex: "All systems go."

Lisa: "Nice. Hope it goes well. Bye."

So, Tuesday rolls around. Alex's excited for his date, as he had already arranged his work schedule to give him only one today and five that Thursday. So, he got to leave work early to finish his prep. Upon getting home, however, Alex realizes there's not much else to do. So, he double checked the times (film showing at 4:30 for a two-hour, seven-minute movie and dinner reservations at 7:00). Seeing as it's only 3:41, Alex mentally high fives himself and repeats his morning routine of 100 pushups, 100 sit-ups, and 20 pull-ups on the pull-up bar bolted into the doorway to his room.

Alex leaves his house, as the clock strikes four. He owned a grandfather clock, because, well, he's old school.

Marguerita lives close. So, Alex finds her house without a problem. He pulls up and walks to the door. Just as he reaches for the doorbell, a gorgeous, petite, Hispanic woman opens the door to greet him.

Marguerita: "Well, heeellllooooo, Alex!"

Alex: "Well, aren't you super anxious?! Valenteen, I take it?"

Marguerita: "Actually, it's Valentee nah. Valenteen is a male name. Seeing as I am not a male, I am not Valenteen. Correct me if I'm wrong, but, word on the street is that you are way too good looking to not want Valentee *nah*."

There is a long silence.

Marguerita: "Well?"

Another long silence.

Marguerita reaches to close the door. Alex sticks his foot in the doorway.

Alex defends his speechlessness. "You directed me to 'correct you if you're wrong.' I am—in fact—way too good looking to not want you. Thus, you are not wrong."

Marguerita giggles. "You're welcome for that setup."

Alex: "Aaawww. You're too kind. Well, shall we skedaddle to the film?"

Marguerita: "Sure."

The two hop in Alex's car to head over to the nearby theater. Alex deliberately has the car radio on a Spanish channel. Marguerita cringes and frowns slightly when she recognizes the maracas of the Hispanic music.

She pleads: "Mind if I turn off the music?"

Alex asks: "I'da thunk you'd like the Hispanic tunes. No?"

Marguerita: "No, it's fine. Just that particular one kinda … rubs me the wrong way."

Alex mumbles to himself: *That's curious.*

Alex shrugs his shoulders and states—aloud—to Marguerita: "Fair enough. To each her own."

Upon arriving at the theater, Marguerita glances at her wristwatch.

"Oh, we're quite early. What time's the movie start?"

Alex: "It'll start whenever I get there." He winks a la *The Godfather*. "I took care of it."

Marguerita gasps: "¡Oh dios mío! So, am I now an… She makes air quotes with her fingers. "*Accomplice?*"

Alex: "Reee lax, babe! As the known, local film critic, I call ahead whenever I'm gonna be here. And, the staff here makes sure I'm happy."

He hands Marguerita a pad of paper and pen.

"Here. During the movie, would you please just occasionally jot down a few notes? So, it seeeeems like we're working. I've just gotta cover my ass. Thanks."

The two stroll into the theater. Marguerita asks for popcorn. Alex refuses. She asks for an icee. He refuses. She asks for a hot dog. Alex shakes his head.

Marguerita: "What's with the refreshment Naziism?"

Alex: "I am thinkin' of our long-term goal of a hearty dinner. I worry that if you snack now, you won't enjoy your meal later."

Marguerita: "Well, I'd like to think that I possess these little things called control and restraint."

Marguerita wants to defiantly stick out her tongue at Alex. But, she resists. She buys a small popcorn, a jujube candy, and a small coke with her own money.

The two then enter the specific room for their 4:30 show.

Marguerita: "I'm on the edge of my seat. What are we seein'?"

Alex: "I arranged for a special showing of the 1997 film, *Selena*. Classic!"

Alex eyed Marguerita more than he actually watched the movie. Probably 'cuz he'd already seen the film for work.

He thinks: "Uh oh. Marguerita looks like she's not enjoying this! I wonder why!"

After the movie, the two walk to Alex's car. As they prepare to leave for dinner, Alex inquires:

"You did not seem to enjoy that film. Like at all. Why was that? Was it something I did?!"

Marguerita smiles politely. But, inside she ain't happy.

"Actually, no. But, kinda yeah. Ya see, members of the Hispanic community do not all hail from the same country, or even from the same region! Selena? She was Mexican. That music in your car? It had maracas. They are Puerto Rican. Specifically, by the Taino Indians. I am Peruvian. Totally different … continent! In lieu of all that, I've kinda lost my appetite."

Alex: "Ah, crud! I'm terribly sorry! Do you still wanna go to dinner?"

Marguerita sighs audibly. "Actually, I'm thinkin', 'Thanks. But, no thanks.' Can you take me back home?"

Alex sighs. "I am so, so, sssooooo sorry! I've become the hypocrite I despise."

Alex hates how people just assume he's a devout Jew from his last name. But, his parents divorced, when Alex was young. He was raised by his agnostic mother. So, his non-religious background came more from nurture than nature. "I thought I was just over preparing. Turns out 'tis …"

Marguerita: "… a form of racism. Specifically, anti-ethicism against the Hispanic community."

Alex drives up to Marguerita's house. He walks her to her door. Alex thanks her for a nice evening.

"I'm sorry we didn't click. We tried. But, mathematically, we're just not like terms."

Alex leans in to give her a farewell kiss on the cheek. Instead, Marguerita grabs him by the shoulders and pulls his face in to hers for an intense, saliva-soaked lip lock.

She's thinking, *I'll make him covet what he ain't gettin'!*

Alex's completely taken aback by this unexpected display of affection. But, his physical mind won out over his psychological conscience. So, he kissed back. With extra tongue to let her taste what she's leavin'.

Set 'em Up. Knock 'em Down

Alex earnestly regrets having to tell Lisa about Marguerita's dismissal of him. But, he takes solace and amusement in the saying: "If you wanna complete some marathons, you're gonna hafta chafe a couple nipples."

Lisa—on the phone—to Alex: "So, … how did it gooooooo?!"

Alex: "Actually, I blew it. Hardcore. She called me out on my ethnically profiling her Latina likes. I'll take full responsibility."

Lisa sighs audibly. "Medically, that's called foot in mouth disease. Ouch! So, next victim?"

Alex: Life is made up of a series of choices. And, life, Lisa, understandably, chose against me. I messed up. So, please."

Lisa fingers through her notes.

"Okay, got one. Natalie's tall, brown hair, brown eyes with great conversation skills. She's a high school guidance counselor. And, I've already talked to her about potential meeting times. She's free any Friday. So, this Friday evening? I'll email you her address. Then, you can email me times. I take it you're tryin' that movie and dinner play?

Alex: "Hey, if it ain't broke, don't fix it. Right?"

Why Change a Good Thing?

So, Friday afternoon arrives. Alex strategically minimizes his Friday workload to allow extra home time for date prep. He makes sure to thoroughly rinse with mouthwash, as Lisa noted that Natalie's a great conversationalist. Plus, he loves this film. So, he could just blather on about it. Hopefully, he does not.

Alex pulls up to her home a little before 4:00 pm. He rings the doorbell. A tall, statuesque beauty opens the door.

Alex snaps his neck in a slack jawed double take. "Wowza!"

Natalie giggles and smiles coyly.

"So, you like what you see? Well…" She looks him up, from his well-kept hair down to his business casual loafer shoes. "… the feeling is mutual."

Alex: "Fantastic start!"

Natalie: "Well, would you like to come in, or do we hafta hurry off to the movie? What time's the movie start?"

Alex—very matter of factly: "Whenever I get there."

Natalie: "So, whenever you specifically arrive, they start a particular movie?"

Alex: "That I pre-selected."

Natalie: "Seriously? How'd you arrange that?!"

Alex smiles slyly. "I have my waaays."

Natalie gives him a tour of the house. They have to wade through scattered clothes and strewn books and actual silverware—three spoons—on the floor.

Alex sees the cutlery and sarcastically inquires: "Ooo, are we having high tea with the Havertons? Aaawww, skiddlywinks! I neglected to bring my new beret!"

Natalie giggles. She plays along.

"No, honey. The Haverton tea party is next week. Remember? Ring for Sedgewick and awsk."

Alex chuckles at Natalie's response, then he turns more serious. "So, why the disheveled living room? Did you just move in?"

Natalie: "Yeah, I did. About four years ago. I just like livin' by the seat o' my pants! Order's boring to me."

Alex: "Aaahhh, I've gotta agree to disagree with you there. But, to each her own. If it works for you, then, by all means, let 'er fly."

Natalie: "I like freedom and independence. Here, do you listen to music? My theme song is Fleetwood Mac's *Go Your Own Way*."

Alex: "No, I do not listen to much music on a regular basis. But, I am familiar with the great song. Look, I'm lovin' how laid back our shmoozin' is. But, do you wanna catch this movie?"

Natalie: "Actually, I think we're really connectin' here—socially. I like it! So, would you hate it, if I wanted to stay in, watch a movie and order a pizza?"

Alex: "... With me?"

Natalie (mimicking Doug Butabi from *A Night at The Roxbury*): "Nooooo. Yeeeeesssss!"

Alex laughs uproariously! "Excellent reference! And, no. I wouldn't mind in the slightest. I just have to make one phone call."

Alex calls the theater to let them know he will not be in attendance tonight. After the two order a pizza but before they pop in a film, they converse.

Alex: "Well, let's begin with our respective backgrounds. Education wise, I attended Harvard. I majored in biomedical engineering."

Natalie: "Whoa!" She giggles. "Did the application form for that major come with complementary braces and wedgies?"

Alex: "Ha ha ha! Uuummm, Negative. It's Harvard, so we were all nerds. No, I actually had to apply separately for a Melvin with an atomic wedgie as a possible substitute."

Natalie: "Jeez! That's some intense hazing. I can't imagine the frat life!"

Alex: "Naw, the Greek system is just not my bag. Too much judging. Acceptance. Denial. It'd be like dating 20 guys. I get enough frustration just from just bein' one!"

Natalie: "Jeeeeez. Dating 20 guys?! Plus, you'd be a huuuuuge slut! I'd definitely call you a whore. Behind your back."

Alex: "I'd call myself a whore! To my face!"

Natalie: "'To your face? What, would you be looking in a mirror?"

Alex chuckles. "I was using sarcasm to be facetious."

Natalie giggles. "I know. I'm being an ass."

Alex: "It's all good. I actually love asses!"

Again, Natalie giggles. This time, she accompanies it with a coy smile.

"Note to self: give Alex a hard time."

The two exchange winks. Alex chuckles, as he gently rubs her calf.

Alex: "Plus, if I were a man whore, that would imply that I'd be paid. I have seen zero dollars of that date money. Ever."

Natalie: "Well, I think that … companionship only requires a monetary exchange after the physical act of sexual intercourse has been completed. Thus, if you did not make love to these men—as you resoundly deny, then you would not have said money."

Alex: "So, we're in agreement. I am a heterosexual non gigolo and have never been and whatnot."

Natalie: "Weeeell, I have my doubts." She giggles coyly.

Confirmation Needed

Alex acts faux upset at Natalie's pretended doubt of his heterosexuality.

He demands: "What, you wanna check my pockets?! Are you questioning my straight ness?!"

Just then, the delivery guy arrives with the pizza. Natalie answers the door. She grabs two plates, two napkins and two Cokes. She returns to the couch.

Alex—to Natalie: "So, you still doubting my hetero-ness?!"

Natalie cringes and nods slowly.

"Trivia test. On only feminine issues! Okay. ... what god, in classical mythology, dressed as a woman, spun wool, and performed other womanly tasks for three years to appease his fellow gods?"

After a minute or two pondering, Alex answers, "Hercules?"

Natalie: "Damnit! Yes. What was the name of the movie that Dustin Hoffman made where he played an actor who pretends to be a woman?"

Almost immediately, Alex replies with *"Tootsie!"*

Natalie: "Who was the first woman in Italy to be awarded a degree in medicine?

Alex: "Hhhmmm. ... Maria Montessori?"

Natalie sighs in frustration. "How do you know all this? Unleeeehhhhhess, you secretly *are* a woman."

Alex: "Well. One, I'm really smart. Two, I am a film critic by occupation. Three, I have my college degree in biomedical engineering. Or, four—all of the above."

Natalie: "Well, since I know two and three to be true, then that implies one to also be correct. Ergo, I'm goin' with option number four. Yes?"

Alex bows. "I applaud your deduction."

Natalie unbuckles the top couple buttons of her blouse.

"According to the kids, 'Smart is the new sexy.' I'm gonna hafta agree."

Alex is oblivious to the intent of her clothing shedding.

"Are you too warm? Where's your thermostat? I'll turn down the heat. Here, the ideal house temperature when eating is sixty-eight degrees Fahrenheit. That'd be twenty degrees Celsius, since you're European."

Natalie: "I'm not European! I'm Oregonian! Actually, every guy thinks I'm Brazilian."

Alex: "Haaarumpf! Oh, I know all too well to not assume a woman's ethnicity." He makes a sad face. "Jeez! Your house was set to eighty-two degrees! Are you tryin' to sweat to cut weight for wrestling? Not that you'd need to at all! Did Lisa tell you I used to wrestle?"

Natalie's growing frustrated and more and more eager: "Yes. She did." She tries to change the subject back to about her. "Hhhmmm. I wonder why heterosexual men would just assume I'm Brazilian. I'm clueless as to why."

She winks at Alex.

Alex—still oblivious: "'I don't get it. Did my hair get flat? Did I stumble into some bad lighting? What's wrong with me?'"

Natalie: "From my current standpoint, ... Not much!"

Natalie hushed: "Except reading between the lines!" She smiles big.

Alex chuckles. "No, silly goose! I was just quoting Cher from the movie, *Clueless* 'cuz you just said you were 'clueless'."

Natalie under her breath: "Right now, you are 'clueless', Alex!"

Alex: "So, should we watch a movie, while we eat?"

Natalie: "Actually, I like our rapport. Would you mind if we just talked?"

Alex: "Not at all, actually. I watch enough movies at work. Just talking is a welcome change of pace."

Natalie giggles. When Alex asks about the pizza, Natalie's extreme frustration erupts.

Natalie: "Come here, and help me reach that container of parmesan cheese on that high shelf. You lift me from behind, while I reach for it."

Alex sighs. "Why don't you just use a chair?"

Better than Pizza?

Natalie has Alex right where she wanted him: with both his hands cupping on and firmly supporting her upper hamstrings. She was relishing the fact that Alex loves a plump behind!

Natalie mumbles—under her breath: "He actually said, and I'll quote—'I actually love asses!'"

Natalie was congratulating herself—in her mind—at her current position. She stalls by pretending to not see the parmesan cheese.

"I just had it! Damnit!"

Alex: "Oh, don't worry about it. I certainly don't need it! Here, hop down."

Natalie: "No, nonsense! It's up here somewhere. Just keep holdin' me. Please! Do not drop me."

She hopes that the countless lunges and squats she randomly does were paying off in terms of strengthening and smoothening her thighs.

Alex: "Don't fret. I will not let you go."

After seven total minutes of lifted searching, Natalie finally grabs the unopened parmesan cheese. Alex slowly lowers Natalie to the floor. He's ambivalent about what just happened:

On one hand, how can it take you that long to find an oft used food in your own house? On the other, I am by no means complainin' about my extensive time cuppin' her gluteus maximus extraordinarius.

As they walk to the couch, Alex hesitantly determines that Natalie should know how he feels about her and her body.

"Natalie, I've gotta get this off my chest. As I'm sure you know. *Incredibili vos habere blandeque coruscant.*"

He exhales a deep sigh of relief, because he admitted his obsession. She looks confused and uneasy.
Natalie: "Was that, like, … olde English?"
Alex: "Oh! That was Latin."
Natalie has a curious and impatient look on her face.
Alex: "Oh! Translated tooooo—You have an extraordinary butt."
Natalie: "Finally! I've been tryin' to get you to notice my rear all night! I've never worked so hard! Well, actually, that's a lie. There was that one kid who just refused to select either his academic prominence or his athletic dominance."
Alex: "Sounds like my adolescence. Why'd he hafta choose one or the other?"
Natalie: "Time management. He just could not balance his time between the classroom and the basketball court."
Alex: "Did you tell him to 'suck it up'? That's what I did."
Exasperated Natalie: "Alright. Enough with this school talk! This is not a parent teacher conference. It's a date! Cuh'meer!"
She reaches across the couch, grabs Alex by the collar and pulls his face in for a kiss. But, she soon pushes him away, 'cuz (ssssshhhhh!) she really likes to sexually tease!
Alex's increasing testosterone and cascading blood into his groin brought him to full attention for the seemingly imminent action. *As Alex insatiably licked Natalie's tongue with his, he wondered,*

Shit! I don't think I planned tomorrow's martial arts class. I cannot just leave the kids hangin'! Besides, I am utterly horrified by the setting of this smelly couch in this messy house. But,—Alex glances down at his phallus—*it obviously feels good. Plus, has she been sneakin' spinach or androstenedione? 'Cuz I cannot overpower her!* Awkward pause. Should I even be thinkin' about innocence and depredation, regardless of which side I'm on?"

Lo and behold, Alex—eventually—slept soundly in a foreign bed. His eventful night was a dramatic interpretation of the movie, *Shaft*. As he lay in bed next to Natalie, he quoted Shaft and triumphantly thought, *You know me. It's my duty ... to please that booty!* But, then, he glanced around at the utter filth, refuse and—worst of all—disorder in just Natalie's bedroom. Alex dared not to think about the rest of the house, 'cuz he could already taste vomit in his mouth. Nonetheless, he arose to sneak to the bathroom to urinate. Talking to himself as he released a deluge of urine into Natalie's toilet, Alex contemplated: *How did I fall asleep last night without first peeing out the added genital arousal?*

Ya see, Alex's urinating conundrum is that sexual stimulation can put pressure on your bladder and/or urethra.

Alex has never had said urine coitus mix-up. but, sometimes, he just feels that he knows too much! It's a double-edged sword, so to speak. He likes to impress. But, he doesn't like to worry about hypotheticals.

Accidentally, Alex reflects—to himself: *What if I pee on (in? Eeew!) My date? What if I meet a woman who knows movies better than I? Would I feel threatened? What if a date discovers a fear of mine I did not know of? What if I—again—offend a date with my poor decision making? Could I recover? Would I wanna?*

WORRY?!

In the morning, Alex and Natalie part ways cordially. First, Alex thanks her for a great night. Embarrassed, Natalie giggles and insists he doesn't need to thank her, "Just for the non sex."

Alex: "I insist! I don't know why. But, the ladies are just not feelin' me! Yes, pun intended. But, you did! And, I hope you enjoyed it."

Natalie: "I did! Maybe I'll call you next week."

Alex: "Don't mess with the maybe, baby."

He enters his car and drives away.

When Alex gets home, he inhales deeply and exhales slowly to relax and calm himself. He spends his entire weekend just relaxing and thinking about future dates. He relaxes so much, that he completely forgets to check his blood pressure. Ever the worrier, Alex startles up a suffocating cloud of apprehension. Strangely, Alex feels hesitant about a potential new relationship. He decides to buy a blood pressure cuff on the way to work, bring it in and test himself there.

Through only intense visual concentration on the sphygmomanometer, Alex can now raise and lower his own blood pressure. Wow. What focus!

Alex's coworker, Peter Simmons, notes to Alex: "Why the heck would you want to raise your blood pressure?"

Alex calmly replies: "So, I can lower it. My body's so topsy-turvy that

I like to play games with it; to test it."

Alex's cell phone rings. As if she could hear his thoughts, Lisa wants to know how the date went.

Alex excited, tells her that it was great. "However, Natalie's really messy. And, it's not like she wants to change. She actually likes disorder. I'm just not sure I can deal with that. I think she's more of a friend. For now depending on how many or how few affectionate connections I end up with. Speaking of which, I'd like to re visit some o' my goodies. Sooooo, I'm thinkin', start over with that girl, Teresa."

Lisa: "Teresa Bethstien? Great. I've always liked her. If at first you don't succeed, try, try again. I hope you two click better this time!"

Alex: "As do I."

Lisa: "Did you not get her number?" Snort of derision. "Amateur. I'll text her."

Alex: "Great. Thanks. So, you're like a good third wheel? So, let me get this straight. By admitting that you've 'liked' Teresa for a long time, are you implying that if Teresa and I get together, you'd wanna jump in to be that—literal—third wheel?!"

Awkward silence.

Lisa: "Uuuuummmmm, … no. So, when would you like to see Teresa?"

Alex: "Hey, a guy can try, right? Actually, how 'bout you just text me Teresa's phone number?"

Lisa: "That way, you're eliminating the middleman. Perfect!"

Dust Yourself off, and Try Again

When Alex gets home that pre-evening,[15] he rushes to check his email.

Sure enough, Lisa came through with Teresa's contact info. He decides to call Teresa, before starting his post work routine.

Alex: "'Sup, Teresa? 'member me, Alex?"

Teresa: "Hello, Alex? I think?"

Alex: "Come ooonnn! You remember me? Alex Kalatovski? We saw *Caddyshack* then enjoyed a quiet dinner."

Teresa scrunches her face, as she's befuddled, until she hears of *Caddyshack*.

"Oh, yeah! That goofy golf movie! And, you had all your bitches in the theater!"

Alex scrunches his face, as he's now befuddled.

"Correct me, if I'm wrong. But, I was under the impression that females dislike the term 'bitches'."

Teresa: "Oh, we do. We do! It's derogatory, inappropriate, and just mean. But, if it's used to disparage men, then that's just amusing."

Alex frowned internally on account of Teresa's double standard.

"By the same token, can a woman be a 'bastard'?"

Teresa: "Actually, yes. Ya see, the term bastard is frequently

---

[15] = pre evening ... but post afternoon

misunderstood. Misconstrued as a fatherless male. But, Webster's dictionary actually defines the term as 'an illegitimate child,' with no gender specification. Sooooo, yes, she can."

Alex: "So, when may I take you out to just dinner, no show?"

Teresa makes an audible sigh. "I suppose that'll work. Just to warn you. I will be saddened by your lack of underlings."

Alex: "Great. How 'bout I take you out to just dinner tomorrow night at about 6:30?"

Teresa: "Aw, shucks! I mean. That'd be great. What type of restaurant?"

Alex sticks with his guns.

"It's a Mediterranean restaurant. So, there'll be alotta lean proteins like chicken or fish, fresh veggies and alotta olive oil.

Teresa: "Mmmmm mmm! Sounds lovely. So, you'll pick me up tomorrow night at around 6:30?"

Alex: "Yes, ma'am."

Teresa: "Yay! I'll have 'bows in my hair.'"

She giggles.

Alex prepares for his date from the night before. He shaves. Personally, he thinks he looks damn gooooood with a 5 o'clock shadow. Alex's face can become rather hirsute. He calls the restaurant to make a reservation. He picks out his clothes.

Should I wear a suit jacket? Why not? I'm having a date. 'Tis a celebratory occasion.

As Alex tries on his jacket, he feels a folded note in the jacket pocket. It has a phone number with Maria written under it.

Noice, thought Alex. He sets the note down on his dresser by the phone. Feeling as if everything's set for tomorrow evening, Alex relaxes enough to watch some SportsCenter and hit the hay.

Alex coasts through a rather uneventful workday. 'Tis his standard operating procedure. View three movies, type up their respective critiques, plan out next workday's schedule. His facial hair foresight is confirmed by his receiving five compliments from four different women on his appearance. When Pocket Simon expresses his admiration of Alex's "facial work", Alex takes him aside to jokingly scold him.

"Dude, your diction… You like my 'facial work'? You just made it weird. Ha ha!"

Alex slaps Peter on the back.

Peter: "Relax, dude! No one's gonna put two and two together on that."

Alex: "Ha ha ha! With my stunning good looks and your inexplicable idolatry of me, the kids are talkin'. Ha ha ha!"

Peter: "So, how can I make 'em think otherwise?! Here, I'm gonna punch you."

Without any hesitation, Peter thrusts a hook punch—with his right hand—at Alex's head. Instinctively, Alex thrusts his own left hand left at eye level to block Peter's strike. Next, Alex slides left hand down Peter's arm to grasp his right wrist. Alex further grasps Peter'a right wrist with his own right hand. Alex raises both his own hands—and, thus, Peter's right arm—above his own head. Alex shuffle steps under Peter's raised arm and rotates around to Peter's back. Alex's still clutching Peter's right wrist. When Alex gets behind Peter, he pins Peter's right wrist to his back and slowly raises it up along his vertebrae.

As Peter writhes and groans in pain, Alex whispers in his ear: "This was just supposed to be a joke. So, why'd you swing at my face? You brought this on yourself." After Peter whimpers out an apology, Alex lets him go. Alex rifles through his pockets, finds a quarter, flips it to Peter and quotes the classic movie, *Home Alone*. "Keep the chaaange, ya filthy animal."

Confidence Is Key

After his demonstration of takin' charge at work, Alex is really feelin' like hot shit, so to speak. Comfortable with his appearance and the restaurant setup, Alex drives over to pick up Teresa. As knowledgeable as he is regarding cinematography, Alex can barely hold in his excitement about just conversing to learn each other's likes and joys. Plus, there's nothing wrong with impressing a date with cultural knowledge. Alex foresees Teresa's amazement with his comfort with the Mediterranean language, food, and customs.

Alex pulls into Teresa's driveway. He doesn't think anything of the three other cars in Teresa's driveway. He's amazed to see Teresa's not only just strolling onto her porch, but all dolled up in a low cut dress and lots of black mascara.

Teresa: "Hey, babe. 'Sup?"

Alex: "Wowza! Look at you. All ooo la la!"

Teresa: "I'm glad you like what you see, 'cuz I'm really tired. Boo hoo! Single tear. Right? How 'bout we just stay in, vej and chat? Would you hate me?"

The two enter the house. The chaotic furniture jumble reminds Alex why Teresa is not at the top of his dating list. She is a beauty but ridiculously messy.

Alex: "Jeeeeeez, no! Everyone's entitled to a break once in awhile. I am perfectly okay with staying in and just talking. I am just wondering.

Why, on earth, would you make yourself so, so, ... sssooooo pretty just to stay indoors?"

Teresa: "Well, I wasn't going to bail out of our date. I wanted to look good for you! Can't that be enough?" She enters her bedroom and closes the door behind her.

Alex: "Oookaaay. So, how do you wanna play this?"

Teresa: "Can we stay in, order food, chat and play here?"

Alex grabs a seat in the kitchen: "Hhhmmm. We can, ... and we may! From where'd you wanna order food?"

Teresa debated internally about whether to disclose what she really wanted to do with the food.

But, "The night is young," she mumbled.

Teresa smiled coyly and said aloud: "My sweet tooth's kinda cravin' some syrupy stuff."

Alex still didn't connect the dots about Teresa's intimate intent.

"'Syrupy'? You got extra napkins ... For cleanup?"

Teresa's playing dumb. "Uuuuummm. We'll make do. I'm more craving a dessert. Do ya mind?"

Alex: "No, ma'am. This is your party! I'm just here to spike aesthetic appeal."

Teresa emerges from her bedroom. She's wearing only a big smile on her face. Alex is pleasantly surprised and overjoyed. To be polite, however, he shuts his eyes and shields 'em.

Embarrassed, Alex lays his other arm over his lap ... to hide his excitement.

Teresa: "Well? 'Aesthetic appeal'? You've clearly got that one covered. Nicely done."

Alex: "You're not so bad yourself."

She signals with her index finger for Alex to follow her into her bedroom. "I dare you to come here."

Alex inhales deeply. He's so happy about his evening plans, that he kinda skips into Teresa's bedroom. Without looking around and assessing the situation, Alex immediately kicks off his shoes and has his shirt halfway off before pausing to catch his breath. He does not look up to see the three naked women—plus naked Teresa—randomly seated in Teresa's room.

Alex now looks around at the beauties, gulps loudly and awkwardly stutters:

"Whoa! It's a g-g-good thing I d-di-didn't wear my t-tih-tie. I'd'a been slightly overdressed!"

He nervously tries to chuckle.

Teresa chimes in: "Oh, yeah! Alex, I meant to tell you, that I'm in a nudist colony. And, these are a few of my friends. They were just leaving. I'll order dinner for just the two of us."

Teresa and Alex leave the friends in Teresa's room. The three ladies dress themselves in their minimalist outfits. They wear just enough to communicate they wear clothes only under duress. Only because society has criminalized public nudism. Each exits to her respective car and departs. Teresa calls and orders two dinners with extra dessert. She walks in on Alex's lying down on the living room couch. He seems to be hyperventilating. But, he's just doing his slow breathing technique to calm himself.

But, Teresa doesn't know about Alex's breathing technique. So, she straddles him and begins mouth to mouth resuscitation. Alex's so stoked that a gorgeous, naked woman is lip locked on top of him, that he cannot maintain his charade very long. He lifts his hands against Teresa's upper back and lightly nudges the back of her head in closer and kisses back. Startled, Teresa lets out a muffled yelp before she realizes who's kissing her and how.

Just then, Alex's phone beeps to signal a text message. It's Christina. Alex thinks, *What timing! Is it a sign?*

While they wait for their food to be delivered, the two conduct an extensive conversation about friends with benefits. Alex eats a small dinner and departs. Late.

Dirty Feelings

After Alex's meal, he departs Teresa's dwelling for the night. However, on his way home, Alex was dealing with the stinging pains of ambivalence.

Am I a man whore?! An inamorato, if you will? I should clean up my act. But, I'm not gettin' the best part—the sex! However, I don't really give a shit, 'cuz prostitutes get paid. And, I've seen ... carry the one. ... add a comma. ... exactly ... zero dollars of non-film critic money.

Alex reaches his own house. Outside his front door, he hesitates.

Should I have stayed the night? Damnit! Probably yeah. Shit! Should I have set up another date? Oh, well. Teresa's affinity for disorder is really a turn off. But, her nudist membership is an amazing turn on! Oh, well. If she actually wants another date, then she will call.

Alex tosses and turns all night. He weighs her immeasurable sexiness against her disgusting messiness.

How could I deny constant nudity from a gorgeous woman? Then again, how could I tolerate such a disorderly personality?

Thankfully, the next day is Saturday—a non-workday for Alex. So, he just lounges around all day. In between nap number three and dump number two, Alex has an "ah ha" moment, when he finds his note about Maria. He takes a few minutes to develop a date itinerary before he calls Maria. Just as he's dialing Maria's phone number,[16] he realizes that he should not organize a date based solely on her ethnic background. He shan't repeat his mistakes with Marguerita.

He'll stick to his guns with a Mediterranean restaurant.

Ring. Rrriiinnnggg. Ring.

Maria: "'¿Hola?'"

Alex: "'¡Hola hermosa! Es Alex ... Kalatovski. ¿Te gustaría salir en una fecha conmigo?'"

Maria: "'¡Oh, qué maravilloso! ¿Tu hablas español?'"

Alex: "'Muy poco. Entiendo más de lo que puedo decir.' So, I'd prefer English, ... if that's okay."

His translated response to her inquiry about whether he speaks Spanish: "Very little. I understand more than I can say."

Maria giggles. "You always were ridiculously smart ... for a jock." She giggles. "So, I'd love to go out with you! When?"

Alex: "How 'bout movie and dinner? Friday? I'll pick you up at 5:30 ... Post Meridiem ... Eastern standard time? Call me with any questions."

Maria giggles. "Here's one. Why are you such an ass?"

She again giggles.

Alex: "Um. I plead the fifth."

He gives her his phone number and hangs up.

Just after his conversation, Alex excitedly exclaims to himself: "Noice!" He closes his eyes, inhales deeply, exhales slowly and ponders the date.

Mediterranean dining? Or, Asian dining? Why not my being a lil' selfish once in awhile? Aaah, Mediterranean, it is. Just, no Spanish cuisine! 'Mediterranean' and 'Spanish' are mutually exclusive terms, dumbass.

Alex was particularly happy, 'cuz he made this particular affectionate connection without Lisa's help. This is all Alex!

---

[16] He was about 42.86% through digit typing. (3 out of 7 numbers) (they share an area code.)

Alex—to himself, aloud: "In retrospect, I am hesitant about also organizing a movie date, 'cuz we need to talk."

Alex's psyche is off the wall. So, he takes three showers per day in an effort to cleanse himself of all the random feminine bodily charisma he imagines is on him. Before work, after work, before bed. Consequently, his water bill's rather high, he's buying alotta soap and he's now using body lotion, 'cuz the excessive scrubbing causes chafing.

Natural Pick Me Up

By the time Friday rolls around, Alex has his entire date night arranged. So, no surprises! He will pick her up at 5:30. The two will watch a 133-minute film at 6:00. Although, really, it's whenever they arrive at the theater. They will enjoy a late dinner—that is not time regulated—at the nearby Mediterranean restaurant. Alex's bizarre psyche is somewhat eased by the Mediterranean cultural custom of late-night dining.

When Alex arrives at Maria's house—at 5:32 pm, he's in awe of all the Hispanic commemorations. He kicks himself for not thinking more stereotypically. Some people distance themselves from their heritage—like Marguerita—and some people embrace it. Maria is obviously the latter. Alex sees a busted piñata in Maria's yard. Two carnival masks lay strewn in the yard.

Alex strolls up to the front door and rings the bell. Maria opens the door almost immediately. Upon seeing her with her luscious hair draped over her bare shoulders, dressed in an elegant evening gown, Alex exclaims: "¡Oh mi! ¡Eres hermosa!"

Translated, he merely confirmed Maria's aesthetic appeal:

"Oh, my! You are beautiful!"

Maria: "Aaawww, muchas gracias, querido! ¡Eres muy guapa! ¡Mismo! En un manly tipo de manera.'"

Alex: "Okay. Now, you're speakin' over my head! What does that mean?"

Maria giggles. "I simply stated, "Thanks so much, dear! You're very pretty yourself! In a manly sort of way."

Alex: "Yes! When I was posing in front of my mirror this morning, I was goin' for man pretty."

Maria: "Well, you can check that off your to do list."

She giggles.

Alex tilts his head toward the masks and asks Maria: "Wasn't carnival season a while ago? Eh?"

Maria giggles in amazement: "Wow, yes! Carnival season is actually late January to early March. For lent. And, it usually includes piñatas."

Alex: "Well, next on my to do list is … attend a movie with a gorgeous woman on my arm." He motions toward the door. "Sooooo, shall we?"

Maria: "Gladly."

The two proceed to Alex's car, which he drives the short distance the Mediterranean restaurant nearby. Soon, they pull up to the night's dining location. Maria gleefully recognizes the restaurant.

"How exciting! I always drive by this place, but I've never had 'los juevos' to go in."

Alex chuckles. "Well, I'd hope that you—a female—still lack the masculine external genitalia now. But, speaking more metaphorically, it's an amazing atmosphere with phenomenal food!"

Maria: "Alliteration aside. What's good here?"

The two stroll in. The hostess semi recognizes Alex's familiar face and seats them almost immediately.

Alex: "Before we eat, how 'bout we talk and better get to know each other?"

Maria: "Okay. I'm a secretary in a real estate office … about a 25-minute drive away. I don't miiiind the work. But, I'd much rather not discuss it."

Alex: "I'm a film critic. My *office* is about a ten-minute drive away. But, I'm almost never there for more than an hour, 'cuz I frequent the movie theater. Yet, I'll admit that I cannot tire of 'el cine' on dates, 'cuz of the great company of my date not of my work organization."

Maria: "So, you're implying that you bring many dates here? Am I just some floozy to you? Another notch on your bedpost?"

Alex's tongue tied as for how to respond. He recovers. "Whoa. Whoa. Whoa. Whoa! First of all, I am so desperate for a partner in crime, that I'm operating on a trial and error system. Hence the many dates. Secondly, you're most certainly not just some floozy to me! You're grade-A. Top o' the line floozy!"

Alex pauses. He just realizes that—even in jest—he's still referring to Maria as a floozy.

Thankfully, Maria sees it as just humor. Only after Maria starts giggling, does Alex chuckle at his own joke.

Alex continues: "Thirdly, who actually keeps a tally of his intimate hookups? That's just sad. And finally, I have a waterbed. So, there is no bedpost."

Maria giggles.

"Waterbed, eh? So, no bedpost? Sounds a bit … fishy. I'll hafta check that out later." She smiles then realizes how that sounds and clarifies. "To verify that there are no engraved numbers!"

Alex knows how odd the menu descriptions may seem to the untrained eye. So, he inquires as to what Maria will order.

Alex: "So, what would you like to eat? I'm gonna steer you away from the seafood based on your marine puns."

Maria: "On the contrary! I do enjoy the seven seas."

Alex: "And, the seafood is delightful here! I'm always partial toward the salmon. But, the seafood potpourri is also great, if you're more dangerous."

Just then, their waiter approaches.

Maria to the server: "That seafood potpourri looks delicious! Can we start with an appetizer?"

The waiter nods.

Alex: "Why not? Wow, you seem hungry. How 'bout the *cacik?* And, the *cigar borek?*"

Maria scans the menu.

"Mmmmm, those look delicious! ... and, for my dinner, I'll have the shrimp shish kebabs!"

Alex: "Great choice! I'll have the *doner kebab*. And, we'll also have some *rakı*, two cups of ice water and one empty glass.

Their waiter thanks them and leaves: "*Teşekkür ederim.*"

Maria to Alex: "*Rakı?*"

Alex: "*Rakı*. An unsweetened, occasionally licorice-flavored, alcohol. It's considered the national drink of Turkey—the country represented by this restaurant."

After both Maria and Alex thoroughly enjoy their meals, Maria downs a glass of *rakı*—straight—and comments:

"Wow, I do like that licorice taste. But, it's strong!" She shrugs, mixes a shot with water and gulps it.

As Maria walks up front with the bill, Alex waits behind to leave gratuity then hurries to catch up. Maria announces to him:

"Well, my half came to about twenty bucks. So, here ya go."

Alex: "Nonsense! I've got it. Besides, ... "He glances at the bill for a minute, calculates and states: "Actually, exactly half would be $18.73. Just for shits and giggles, though, I will accept the seventy-three cents."

Maria: "Oookaaaaay. That's beyond odd. Might I ask why?"

Alex: "I'm glad you did. Ya see, of all the known numbers in the world, seventy-three is ... by far the best número."

Maria: "¿Por qué?"

Alex clears his throat and states: "I'm glad you asked. Ya see, seventy-three, *o setenta y tres* is the twenty-first prime number. Its mirror, thirty-seven, is the twelfth and its mirror, twenty-one, is the product of multiplying seven and three. In binary talk, seventy-three is a palindrome. It's 1001001, which backwards is 1001001."

Alex pulls the car up to Maria by the front door. Maria stumbles, as she enters the car.

"Jeez, I thought. I cuh-zzuh-uhd handle my boo oooze."

Alex: "But, you thought wrong. Oh, yeah. I meant to tell you beforehand. *Rakı* is ninety percent alcohol by volume. Time magazine ranked it number five on its list of top ten ridiculously strong drinks."

Alex drives to Maria's house. He walks her to her door. When she has trouble finding the keyhole and doorknob and forgets that it's a pull open door, Alex picks her up. He carries her inside the house and lays her on her bed. He leans over, kisses her cheek, and wishes her "good night and goodbye."

Maria straightens up.

"Nooo, please stay! What do ya want? I'll give you anything!"

She dry heaves a couple times. Alex grabs a trash container. As if by cue, she vomits into it.

Alex's humorously wowed. "What control!"

Maria: "Please stay here with me!" She pats the bed.

Alex sighs audibly. "I'll stay in the room. But, your upchuck reflex is rather unsteady right now. So, I'll leave you this garbage bag and extra space in your bed. But, I will camp out on the floor for the night just to make sure you make it through the night okay."

Maria—clearly disappointed—responds: "Aw, shucks. Well, then would you please help me put on my nightie?"

Alex consents, just as Maria again spews into the garbage can. He hands her a towel to wipe her mouth. She cleans up and removes her shirt. "You gonna help me with my nightie? The garbage can! Quick. ... Quick!"

Alex hands her the receptacle, just as her gastric ejection shows itself.

Alex exclaims, "Whew! What a save!"

Maria picks out some nightwear from a drawer and hands it to Alex. He assists her in undressing then redressing. After she lays down her head and instantly falls asleep, Alex commends himself for resisting the urge to climb in bed with Maria.

Psychological Rights >> Physical Wrongs

Despite upsetting his fragile psyche by trying to sleep in an unfamiliar location, Alex actually sleeps very well on Maria's floor. He fears that he was so comfortable and relaxed, that he ... snored! (Shh! He did.) He knows he has a habit of breathing very heavily and loudly, when he's calm and content. Thankfully Maria was out cold—from the *raki*—and couldn't hear his snorting.

When Maria finally awakens from her booze induced slumber, she runs to her bathroom to relieve her loaded bladder. After urinating and washing her hands, she makes sure to wipe the dried spit up from the corners of her mouth and chin. When Maria exits the bathroom, she's relieved to see that Alex's still here! True to his word, Alex lay curled up with a pillow on the floor. Awake. And staring at Maria, as she walks to and from the bathroom. As she climbs back into bed, she says to Alex, "Heeey, you're still here! Thanks a lot for stayin' with me. I feel much better today." As if on cue, Maria has to run back to the toilet to blow chunks.

Alex sarcastically: "Oh, I can tell. You sound..." Tony the Tiger, 'Frosted Flakes' voice "Gggggrrrrreaaaat! So, now that I see you're still alive, I'm gonna head out. K?"

Maria: "Oh, nooooo! Please stay." She pulls her nightie off her shoulders and bats her eyes wantingly.

Alex turns his head away. "I appreciate the invite. But, I've gotta…" Alex makes air quotes with his fingers. "…feed the monkey!"

Maria: "Oooh! You have a pet ape? How cute! What kind?"

Alex sighs audibly. "Didn't you see my air quotes?" He repeats the two-handed fingers gesture and sighs again. I have this routine in which I watch Sportscenter, as I chow down on the omelet I make. Sooooo, I'm due for some grub and sports. Ya mind if I head out?"

Maria: "Not at all. Thanks a lot for stayin' to be my safety valve."

As Alex grabs his watch and keys to leave, he remembers to give Maria his parting thoughts.

"I'm out. May I please call you soon?"

He leans in to kiss her cheek goodbye. In doing so, Alex leaves his upper body exposed.

Sure enough, Maria grabs him by the collar and pulls his face in for a wet, sloppy lip lock. Only to not be rude, Alex thrusts forward his tongue, when he feels Maria's dancing tongue in his own mouth. Alex really likes the kiss, but he realizes it was probably wrong. Unfortunately for his hyper libido, he sees sexy, beautiful, Maria as more of a friend.

Alex tries to separate himself from Maria's lips. But, surprisingly, Maria overpowers him. Alex is honored by Maria's determined display of affection. But, he soon pulls out[17] of her mouth, when he tastes her leftover vomit.

Maria's confused. "Why not?!"

Alex explains: "It's not that you're not attractive. Believe me, you're beautiful. It's just that my heart is set on another, and I see you as more of a … great friend."

Maria hoping: "With benefits?"

Alex jokingly: "Hey, I can't see the future!"

Alex clasps Maria's hands, leans in, kisses Maria on the cheek and

---

[17] Pardon the unfortunate pun. But, it's what he would—inevitably—have had to, if he let their closeness get that far. But, internally, he hesitantly decreed. "nooo."

bids Maria adieu. She whines and stomps her feet in a little tantrum, as she pleads, "Whyyy?"

Alex figures Maria will be upset with this news, but he knows he must tell her. It's a necessary evil.

Alex: "I previously saw this woman." *Truth.*

"We really connected." *Truth.*

"She contacted me again recently." *Lie.*

"She's not quite as beautiful as you." *Half-truth to make Maria feel better.*

"But, our schedules really match up, and our interests are, like, exactly the same." *Half-truth to make Maria feel better.*

"It's just unfortunate timing. She beat you in the race." *Truth.*

Maria frowns. Alex shrugs and snaps his fingers in a "pishaw" motion. He kisses Maria on the cheek and exits to his car. Finally, he leaves.

Retrieval

Alex sleeps soundly that night. In his own bed. At his own house. When he arises the next morning, he happily but anxiously calls Christina. Remembering that it's now Saturday, Alex relaxes.

He calms himself by internally assuring himself: *There's no church 'til tomorrow.*

The phone rings. And rings. … and rings. Alex grumpily sighs loudly and disappointingly at Christina's non answer. He grimaces, shrugs and vows to try again later. In the meantime, he deduces that it's a good time for a dip. So, he changes into his swim trunks to dive into his swimming pool. After all his commendable athletic achievements, Alex had become slightly full of himself. He loves to swim, as it relieves stress, promotes muscular strength, and reduces back pain.

Alex's previous job—about thirteen years ago—was as an applications analyst for a petroleum distribution company. So, he'd spend 10-hour workdays just hunched over his computer screen, no one to converse with.

In Alex's head, he computed:

Ten-hour work days times five work days per week times fifty yearly work weeks (two weeks annual vacation) times eight years (right outta college) equals twenty-thousand work hours of lumbar stress

He cherished his lavatory breaks. He'd bring lunches with alotta strawberries, almonds, and broccoli, 'cuz he actually wanted many poop breaks to get away from his deskwork. Additionally, he'd pack alotta citrus, spicy foods, and sandwiches with tomatoes to stimulate his bladder.

So, his swimming habit began as back relief but became a regular routine, once Alex saw the positive physical results. He won't admit to being vain or self-absorbed. But, how else would one explain his constant nutrition monitoring plus flexing in front of mirrors?! Alex licks his lips, as he admires the reflections of his bulging pectorals, deltoids, biceps, and triceps. He self compliments his lower body muscles in his body length mirror at home, like his calves, quads, hamstrings and glutes. Plus, he can just feel his stronger core.

Apparently, Alex's self-worshipping is a constant and ongoing procedure. He desperately tries to get others to notice any of his virtues. So, he calculates the cost of dinner bills in his head. He quotes movies at opportunistic times. He armlocks wise asses. He visits known exotic restaurants. But, theology is one topic he knows absolutely zero about. Thus, he hopes to learn more from many outings with his new acquaintance, Christina.

After his swim and subsequent shower, Alex calls Christina again.

After four rings, she finally answers in a calming, feminine voice.

"You rang?"

Alex: "Hey, babe! It's Alex, the gentleman who took you out to that lovely Turkish restaurant, got you all boozed up on some color-changing water-esque liquid called *rakı* and resisted the temptation of taking advantage of you. 'Cuz that would be a despicable sin!"

Christina: "Oh, yeeeah. That was great. I was hoping to see you again."

Alex: "Where were you earlier? I figured, 'cuz it's Saturday, you wouldn't have theological commitments. You weren't seein' another guy, were you?" Alex fakes a sniffle. "I can take rejection."

Christina: "I was teaching Saturday school. For the kids. Actually." She giggles. "There's only one ... sorta man in my life ... up there." She nods her head upward.

Alex half mockingly: "Isn't your … significant other all around us? Is He here? Or, there? Ssshhh! Ya hear that?"

Christina slightly annoyed: "Hear what?"

Alex: "Yep. I think your man just farted. Oh, it's in my eyes!"

Christina giggles again and admits: "Jeeeez. I don't care how old I get, flatulence is always funny."

'Twas like music in Alex's ears. He chuckles. "I couldn't agree more. Can I get an Amen!"

Christina: "Amen! The hilarity of gaseous emissions aside. What's goin' on?"

Alex: "Well, I was wondering, no, hoping that you'd like to venture out with me again. Maybe tonight?"

Christina: "Sure! Why not?"

Alex: "Great! How 'bout we do dinner and a movie this time?"

Christina: "Sounds delightful. Just to warn you, though—I've got early morning church services tomorrow. So, I'll hafta catch some z's early."

Alex: "How early is 'early'?"

Christina: "Well, the first service is at eight, then another one's at eleven. The church is about a ten-minute drive away. So, I've gotta be up and about by about six."

Alex: "Jeeeeez! One hundred ten minutes of prep work. Jeeeeez! You are such a woman! So, how atheist are these kids?"

Christina: "No. Silly goose! It's not that they don't believe. It's more that they don't care. So, the kids—for the most part—are more agnostic. So, I prepare elaborate and entertaining lessons to stimulate their faith."

Alex: "Ah, nice! Ha ha ha! I've got just the movie for us to watch."

Christina: "So, what—might I ask—is the plan?"

Alex: "Since you have an early morning commitment …"

Christina: "Well, it's more than just a 'commitment.' It's my job!"

Alex chuckles: "As I was saying… Since you have an early morning obligation to the kids, how 'bout I pick you up at about three-thirty for a four o'clock movie then a romantic dinner?"

Christina: "Nice and early. Sounds great, thanks! What movie?"

Alex: "Suuurprise!"

Christina sighs. "And the restaurant?"

Alex grins sheepishly: "One where you won't get wasted!"

Christina: "Soooo, anywhere! Could you be more vague?!"

Alex chuckles. "I've got my eye on you. Just wait and see. I'll be there at 3:30."

Alex calls the theater to make sure they'll be ready. He checks out a few biblical sites on the internet to have issues to discuss with Christina. He checked the movie duration one more time, 'cuz he forgot. It's about two hours long. So, dinner will start at about 6:30. Well, since they're goin' to a Spanish restaurant (technically, the owner's a Colombiano.), he reviewed the language on a few academic sites.

He practices: 'Comeremos a las seis y media.'

Once Alex feels content with his Spanish speaking and biblical referencing, he heads out to his car to begin his evening. During his drive, Alex debates whether he should switch his car radio to the AM liturgical music channel. Ruling that Christina prolly gets enough of that at work, Alex decides against the ecumenical selection. He does not apply this same reasoning to his film selection.

It's a comedy. So, there are different rules. She'll laugh it off.

Alex arrives at Christina's house. He rings the bell. As he waits at the door, he again notes the religious… paraphernalia decorating the porch area.

He shrugs and mutters to himself: *Whatever floats your boat.*

Christina answers the door. She's gorgeous! Alex can't help but comment: "Do you keep a stack of hand towels or wipes in your office at work?"

Christina: "Um, no. Why?"

Alex: "The kids' drool." He glances over her again. "Daaaaammmn!"

Christina blushes and kisses Alex on the cheek. Alex's face lights up. He screams, *Score!* internally. A timer rings and Christina turns away to the back area.

She yells back: "Come on in and have a seat. I'm just doin' laundry and puttin' on m' face."

Alex: "Well…" He chuckles. "You've certainly selected a beautiful 'face' for the public."

Alex intends to speak under his breath. But, he's accidentally in an audible voice. Thanks to her sixteen plus years working with soft spoken children, Christina developed extraordinary hearing. She'd even developed an educational transition for when one of her students mumbles how much he hates her and her stupendous hearing:

"You shall not hate your brother in your heart, but you shall reason frankly with your neighbor, lest you incur sin because of him."

— Leviticus 19:17

After a few additional minutes, the two depart for their date.

Good Things Come to Those Who Wait

As the two make their way to their movie viewing, Alex asks about the radio: "Did you want to listen to some tunes? Or, I figured you'd like the theological discussions. … but, then, … I had second thoughts. I'm sure you hear enough theological debate at work. This is supposed to be a relaxing date. Turn off your preaching mind."

Christina: "Please don't just assss oooom you know what I'm thinking or how I'm feeling."

Alex: "A thousand apologies, dear! If it were I, … I'm just sayin' I'd wanna … initiate other neurologic ganglia."

Christina looks confused. She smiles and nods sarcastically.

Alex: "In layman's terms, I'd wanna change it up."

Just then, a rushing doofus driver runs a red light. So, Alex slams on his brakes and instinctively thrusts his right arm straight 90 degrees to protect Christina from whiplash.

He angrily exclaims: "God damnit! What the fuck was he thinkin'!"

Christina gasps. "No no no … no! Just 'cuz a guy's a moron, … that's no excuse for blasphemy. Also, God's last name is not 'damnit'." She blesses him with the sign of the cross. *"In nomine patris et filii et spiritus sancti."*

Alex: "Blessing me with the 'Body of Christ' is like bringing a yardstick to Germany…. it just doesn't belong."

Christina looks confused.

"How so?"

Alex: "Ya see, *die deutschen* are on the metric system. So, they do not understand the concept of yards. I blame Hitler. Anyway, one-meter equals approximately 1.094 yards."

Christina giggles loudly.

"Ya know, there aren't enough Hitler jokes! Yes, he was a very sadistic psychopath who caused some unforgivable pain and grief. But, he's in the past. We move on and try to be happy."

Alex arrives at the theater. He does his usual routine of strolling into the theater, signaling to the staff, buying two drinks then choosing two middle seats in the pre-selected room. Christina giggles and kisses Alex's cheek, when she notices that they will be watching the movie, *Keeping the Faith*.

The two really enjoy the 128-minute film. Alex does not mention that he's already seen the movie. He jokingly lies by telling Christina he had a lavatorial malfunction.

Alex: "Ha ha haaa! Oh, shit. I just laughed so hard, I peed a lil'. I squirted some. You'd think a 43-year-old man would have better bladder control. I mean, I'm not 80! I mean, I'm barely … 53.75% of that!"

Christina: "Eeewwwwweeeee!" She giggles again. "Jeeeeez! You can do math, while you pee?"

Alex: "What can I say? I like to multitask." He makes the motion of wiping the dirt off his shoulder. "Now, we're off to dinner."

Christina: "Yay for me! Where to?'

Alex: "It's a great place. The food's terrific! Just, the host is kind of a dick.… Don't say I didn't warn you."

Alex pulls into his own driveway, … unbeknownst to Christina. After Christina follows Alex inside the front door of the mansion, and after she observes Alex's face in all of the pictures, she finally puts two and two together.

She blurts—with sarcasm just dripping from her lips:

"Jeez, this place is so small, I'm gonna hafta go outside just to change my mind!"

Alex leads her outside—onto the spacious pool patio.

"Second thoughts?"

Christina: "Jeez Louise, this is nice."

Alex: "How do your words taste? Grab a seat."

Christina (sarcastically): "Soooo, where's the host of this little soiree? Word on the grapevine is he's..." Air quotes. "Kind of a dick."

Alex: "Here, you ponder what you want to eat, and I'll go get this 'dick,' as you say."

Alex turns to leave. He makes a "whoosh" sound and faces Christina.

Alex in a deeper voice: "What may I get you to eat?"

Christina: "Wait. The menu?"

Alex: "It's whatever your little heart desires. Jeeez! Who needs a 'menu' for that?"

He quietly mumbles, "It's common frickin' biology."

Alex takes two steps away, turns around, covers his face with his hand, makes a "whoosh" sound to signify his character change and turns back to face Christina.

Alex in a higher voice: "Why, yes, mademoiselle. I am the owner. I apologize for the host. He's a bit rude. Nonetheless, I hope you're having a gay ol' time! So, what's eatin' ya?"

He giggles at his own pun.

Christina: "I just wanted to praise the atmosphere you've got here. It's very sooooothing. I was hoping that you knew the whereabouts of my date. He'll get pissed, if he sees me talkin' to all these other guys. But, what momma don't know won't hurt her, right? Ssshhh!"

Alex as owner: "Um, what's he look like? Or, is it a she?"

Christina: "Well, he is about six feet tall, about ... 200 pounds. He has a ginormous..." She giggles. "...heart. And, he's strikingly handsome."

Alex makes the "whoosh" sound and plops down in the lounge chair next to Christina as Alex.

"Ta daaa! 'Tis I Alex. I was just scopin' out the kitchen crew."

Christina: "Uuuuummmmm, what? You just pretended to be the host and the owner. All you did was change the pitch of your voice. You must think I'm preeehtty stupid!"

Alex: "Au contraire! You're merely half correct: you're very pretty, and I'm kinda stupid."

He frowns an unhappy face.

"So, what would you like for dinner? I'll make you anything."

Christina sarcastically: "What, no menu?"

Alex makes the "whoosh" sound to transform into the deep voiced host: "I do recall the chef's saying 'eh nee thing'."

Christina is pleasantly surprised. But, she's playful and wants to stump him.

"I'll have the eggplant parmigiana."

Alex as waiter: "As you wish. While you wait, might I urge your trying out the ool? Notice that there's no 'p' in it. Staff would like to keep it that way."

Christina: "I didn't bring my suit. Next time."

Alex internally high fives himself, 'cuz Christina just implied that there will be a "next time." Alex pumps his fist and quietly mutters, "Score!"

Alex turns around and makes the "whoosh" sound to transform into the chef.

"Too much socializing and not enough cooking. To the kitchen!"

After about ten minutes of humming and twiddling her thumbs, Christina decides to walk over to the "ool" to check the temperature.

To herself: "Ooooo. Nice and warm."

She doesn't know of Alex's pool heater, that he brilliantly turned on that morning for just this purpose to impress a possible guest.

Mind Changer

Twenty minutes after ordering an eggplant parmigiana, Christina realizes the [necessary] timing. She joyfully skips inside the house and into the kitchen.

"Oh, my goodness! You were serious! A quality eggplant parmigiana takes about four hours of cooking and prep work plus overnight saucing. Can I switch to a twenty-minute baked salmon? For less cooking time and more talking time."

Alex: "Ask and you shall receive. What sides would you like?"

Alex: "Oh, hell! I'll make broccoli with cheese and a baked potato. K?"

Christina: "Wow. Sounds fantastic. 'Mind if we stay in here, and I just watch and talk to you, as you cook?"

Alex: "If you don't mind my seeming to be a lil' out of it, 'cuz I tend to really get into my making taste orgasms. I didn't know you were into voyeurism."

Christina: "Ha ha ha! Are you kidding? This is merely the foreplay."

Alex chuckles. He is ecstatic that someone ... a woman, no less ... finally understands and even furthers his inappropriate humor and sexual puns.

Alex dresses up the salmon with salt, pepper, garlic, rosemary, thyme, parsley and lemon wedges. He puts the four fillets (in case she wants seconds) on a baking sheet in the oven. He sets his kitchen timer for fourteen minutes and washes his hands.

Alex: "Okay. Let's heat things up by headin' out to the grill for the broccoli and potatoes."

Christina: "I love how organized you are."

Alex: "I need order. Almost to the extent that it's a character flaw."

Christina: "Flaw? How so?"

Alex: "Well, there was this one girl I went out with. She was beautiful."

Christina sits slack jawed … with mouth agape. She interjects "Oh, nice. So, you're dating other women? Plus, you think she's 'beautiful'? I'm outta here!"

She throws down her napkin and stands to storm off.

Alex loudly continues, hoping that she'll listen and stop.

"But, she was insanely messy! That was just… unbearable. So, I started anew and met … youuu. Is my search over? Hhhmmm. I know not!"

Christina stops and does a slow about face. She sees Alex's cheek to cheek smile. She rushes over to lock arms with Alex and to plant a long, wet kiss on his lips. She was debating about where to rest her hands, when Alex broke away.

"Gotta watch the food!"

As Alex flips the potatoes and layers the cheese on the broccoli, Christina audibly licks her lips. Alex covertly sees her longing gesture and inquires: "Now, Christina, what is so lip smacking to you? The food? Or … the chef?"

Christina shyly smiles and replies: "Must the two be mutually exclusive?"

Like the nerd he is, Alex's response: "I dig your logistical reasoning!"

Christina: "So, how'd you—a film critic—become so comfortable cooking and grilling for others?"

Alex: "Well, my father was a chef and my mother a waitress. So, I've got the restaurant service in my blood. They never actually sat down with me and taught me. I just learned by watching 'em. I'm a visual learner. So, I'm afraid I'd be a pretty crappy student in your theology classes."

Christina gasps then giggles. "Don't be so hard on yourself. You seem like you pick things up well."

Alex: "Plus, I like to impress. … how am I doin'?"

Just then, the kitchen timer rings. So, Alex removes the broccoli and potatoes from the grill, sets 'em on two big, separate plates and carries 'em into the kitchen. Christina follows him.

Alex's curious. He chuckles.

"I'm about to serve. Why don't you sit and relax? Ha ha ha! Stop followin' me."

Christina: "I like watchin' you work."

Alex: "While you're in here, you could help me serve you." He chuckles. "I'll get you a salmon filet and a tater. You take as much broccoli as you'd like."

Christina thankfully obliges. The two eagerly sit on the patio by the pool, each with a full plate of salmon, baked potato and broccoli. As they sit, Alex hops up, 'cuz he just remembers to serve the wine.

Alex: "Well, not to brag, but I also teach martial arts to kids, and I'm a jujitsu student. So, you'd hafta come watch a class."

Christina: "Jujitsu?"

Alex: "It's ground fighting."

Christina: "And, did you say you teach kids jujitsu classes?"

Alex: "Indeed, I did. Why?"

Christina: "Noice! What if I encourage my kids to go try your class? O'course, I'll hafta go check out the class first. To rate its worth. As an unbiased outsider. Unbiased? Ha! Ha."

Alex: "Grace?"

Christina recites a powerful, love cherishing prayer. Right before they start eating, Alex hands Christina the stereo remote to bless it.

Christina eyes Alex angrily. "Why?!" If looks could kill.

Alex answers. "'Cuz God smiled, when he honored me with your presence."

Alex clicks a button on a remote control, and a song starts playing over the patio loudspeakers. It's ol' school: N'sync's *God Must Have*

Spent A Little More Time on You. Christina gratefully smiles. But, she quickly realizes the error of her ways. Her cute smile quickly turns upside down into a disconcerting frown.

Thankfully, she explains: "At first, I was very appreciative of your compliment. Thanks."

Alex reaches for her hand, squeezes it and mouths, "You earned it."

She continues: "However, I soon remembered the words of the great Saint Augustine, who said, 'It was pride that changed angels into devils. It is humility that makes men as angels.' Are you—Alex Kalatovski—trying to tempt me with one of the seven deadly sins, ... pride?"

Alex looks horror stricken. "'Twas just a compliment! I was trying to be really slick in telling you that I really like you. But, your pessimistic reading between imaginary lines made that just blow up in my face!" He gives an audible sigh.

Christina reverses her delicate emotional state back to happiness again. She smiles and kisses Alex. A few seconds pass of their just staring into each other's eyes, before Alex breaks the silence: "Dig in!"

The two thoroughly enjoy all the food and beverage. Christina even pours herself three more glasses of wine. As Christina's speech begins to slur slightly, Alex jokes: "If that's Christ's blood, then he must've been wasted 24 7, right?"

Christina's head slightly sways back and forth, and she lets out a barely audible but very feminine burp.

Alex: "... Like you are, obviously."

Christina excuses herself for the barely audible burp.

Christina: "What are you taaaaalkin' about?! Our lord, Jeebus Chryse, could hooooold his liquor!"

Alex chuckles. "The opposite of you, right?"

Christina drifts in and out of levelheadedness.

"Wowza! Compliments to the chef. That salmon was pretty scrum dilly umptious! The broccoli? And cheese? Mmm! And, the potato? Mmm! And, the wine?"

Alex is quick to interject. "I can see from your three glasses that you thought the wine was …" He makes a kissing sound, as he pulls his closed fingers away from his lips. Magnifique."

Christina jubilantly leans over to kiss Alex. Looooong and wet.

Alex offers: "Well, that was a faaan tabulous date! How 'bout I drive you home?"

Christina: "But, I wanna swim!"

SHARED INTERESTS

After a rather one-sided debate, Alex drives a stumbling Christina home. He turns on his car radio for a moment. Alex quickly shuts it off, when he realizes that some soothing music may just put inebriated Christina to sleep. He thinks to give her some extra strength Tylenol PM, if her drunkenness goes that far.

But then, Alex worries that she'll be either too sleepy or too jumpy for her services tomorrow—Sunday.

Alex thinks: *She's a grown woman. I dare not ask her exact age! I'm sure she's had her experience with combatting hangovers. Should I stay with Christina tonight to make sure she's alright? Hhhmmm. I don't really have many obligations tomorrow. But, I can't just invite myself over. I've gotta eeease into it. Thankfully, this is one of the weekends I arranged with my martial arts associates to cover for me in teaching the kids' classes. Thus, Christina equals top priority."*

Alex says loudly—to Christina—to keep her awake: "So, Christina, tell me about these kids to whom you preach. You think they'll like jujitsu?"

Christina: "Heck yeah, they will! I mean, they'll be interested. I'll hafta go watch one of your classes to get a better idea of how to explain it."

Alex: "Hey, why don't I do that isplainin'? How 'bout you come watch me teach to first gauge it, then I go to one of your services to formally invite 'em and answer any questions?"

Christina excitedly replies: "That sounds splendid! When do you teach?"

Alex: "I—personally—teach an hour-long kids' class on Tuesday and Thursday evenings from six to seven. Plus, I have an intense two-hour class on Saturday mornings from 10 am to noon. I also make myself available for any questions or private workouts on Sundays. Thinking ahead, I arranged for no workouts tomorrow."

Christina: "May I observe a class this coming Tuesday? Where at?"

Alex: "I've got a nice dojo across the street from the YMCA about ten minutes away."

Christina: "Oh, yeeeah! And, that's down the street from my church!"

Alex: "Um, if you say so, sure! I'm tryin' to make it easy on the parents!"

Christina giggles and rolls her eyes. She half sarcastically states: "Oh, you're sooooo thoughtful!"

Alex: "Oh, aren't you the sweetest? How 'bout you write that down, so you do not forget. I just have this gut feeling that it'll slip your mind." Under his breath: "... since you're drunk". More audibly, "Here. I will write you a note. ... Ssshhh! Don't tell the teacher we're passin' notes."

Christina slowly stumbles over to her notepad on the fridge and shows him where to write.

Alex writes: *Alex Kalatovski. Teaches kids' jujitsu on Tuesdays and Thursdays 6-7 pm and Saturdays 10 am to 12 noon. Go check out for churchgoers.*

He secretly, hurriedly adds a note for Christina, hoping it'll slip into her subconscious:

Alex = damn handsome.

Once finished writing the note, Alex cavorts back into the living room to find Christina lying face up, supine, in the middle of the room, on her floor. He hurries over to roll her onto her stomach to ensure she does not choke on her own vomit. He sits on the couch and waits for Christina to awaken from her drunken stupor. He knows he should not leave Christina by herself in her current inebriated state.

His conscience chimes in: *'Twud be irresponsible and unfriendly.*

At the same time, he struggles to find something to do, 'cuz to wander around would be invasive. So, he made himself comfortable on the couch and popped on the television. She's gotta, at least, have some water to better prevent a hangover.

Seconds to minutes to hours went by. But, still, there is little to no movement made by Christina. Almost on cue, she would incessantly heave and spit up some of her dinner about every ten minutes.

Alex's dominant more scientific left brain interjects: "Actually, doofus. Christina regurgitates after eight minutes and forty-seven seconds, then after nine minutes and

twenty-two seconds and after eleven minutes and eight seconds. That's one vomit per every approximately 9.83 minutes. C'mon, man! You're dealing with someone's life! You've gotta be more exact than that lazy 'about ten minutes' crap!

Alex lets out an audible sigh when he realizes it's approaching midnight. He tries to rustle Christina from her deep, intoxicated snooze. Nothin' doin'. He knows he shouldn't just leave her. But, on a typical date, they'd have parted ways long ago. So, technically, his responsibility is done. But, he knows he should stay to help care her back to health. So, he carries her into her bedroom and lays her, face down, on her bed. Alex tries to be loud in his slamming clothes drawers, occasional forced coughing and deliberate stumbling. She still does not stir. Alex sighs again. He debates about whether to undress her and redress her in her nighty.

Hhhmmm as much as he wanted to help, he decides against the act, 'cuz it'd probably misinterpreted as inappropriate. All the while, Alex keeps a wastebasket and towel nearby, as Christina's vomiting remains timely like clockwork. Nonetheless, Alex sleeps soundly, as he lies alongside Christina in her bed.

Having forgotten what time Christina said she arose for her church services, Alex just sets Christina's alarm for an early 6:00 am on a weekend. He sets his watch alarm for 5:45 am, so he can start to get stuff ready for her day. Upon his watch's beeping, Alex rolls over to surreptitiously snuggle with Christina. He's being the big spoon. Alex awakens in a great mood, 'cuz he's still so happy with how his date went last night. Soon, he remembers that he's morally obligated to getting Christina started that morning. So, he hops up to check her alarm clock for timing and to check her closet for evangelical clothes. What those looked like, Alex hasn't the slightest idea. So, he just sets out a robe and a fancy dress he finds. Next, Alex moves to the kitchen, because he figures to make her some breakfast. He scopes out her refrigerator contents and her cooking appliances for his breakfast prep.

Just as he reaches for a few eggs to make an omelet, he has second thoughts: "Hhhmmm. Christina's going to church, and she may or may not have to speak aloud extensively. So, would eggs be good for her? Hhhmmm."

Alex pauses before continuing. "Why yes. Eggs contain high amounts of B vitamins. And, here, I'll put many tomatoes in 'em. What else?" He notes some assorted do's and don'ts, as he creates a medically beneficial morning snack for the weakened. With his supersonic hearing, Alex hears Christina's alarm's buzzing. So, he tiptoes to her bedroom to assure her he's not a burglar and to calm her.

Christina's unfazed by the alarm's noise, as she's still in a deep slumber. Alex sits on the bed. As she's still lying face down with her head tilted to her left to prevent her drowning in her own vomit, Alex realizes that he should step in. He gently nudges her a few times, as he calls out her name.

"Christiiiiina. … Cccrrriiiiisssttteeeeeeennnaaa."

Alex could feel himself beginning to nod off. Sooo, he stops that.

"To hell with that idea. Fuck it."

Alex immediately raises a hand over his mouth and bites his lip. Something about this house makes him very self-conscious of blasphemy and cursing. Is it Christina's aura as a priest for children?

Alex is in awe: "Holy shi … I mean. … wow! She's gooood!"

Alex holds her hands, as he leans in to slowly kiss her lips. Then, as if she were electrocuted, Christina immediately shoots up with excitement and confusion.

"What happened? Where am I? … What day is it? … What time is it?!"

Alex calms her. "Sssssshhhhh. Reeelax. The two of us went on a date. We saw the ol' timer movie, *Keeping the Faith*. Then, I made you dinner at my house. You were having such a great time, that you drank a few too many glasses of wine, and they got to you. I drove you to your house where we are now. But, you were way too drunk for me to just leave you alone. I hope you don't mind, that I'm still here. I'm making you breakfast."

Christina: "Or, did I drink a lot as an emotional crutch during a bad date?"

Alex: "Nonsense!"

Alex leans up to get outta the bed. Christina clotheslines him to make him lie back down.

"'Nonsense? If what you say is true, then I owe you my thanks. What can I give you? Anything."

Alex rubs his chin, as he ponders.

"Hhhmmm. A second date? And, your enjoying my breakfast."

Christina: "Deal! Did you really make me breakfast?"

Alex: "Well, I'm in the process of making a meal that would be beneficial to your talking to a group. 'Cuz it's Sunday today. Church day."

Christina: "Fabulous! Ya mind if I watch you cook?"

Alex: "That'd be great. Plus, you could find stuff for me. But, what of church? The time?"

Christina panics. Then she observes that it's 6:07. She exhales deeply in relief. "The first service is at 8:00, and the other one's at 11. How did you know to wake me at this time?"

Alex: "Well, I listen to people I like. And, I really like you. Ergo, I really listen to you."

Christina: "Wow, what a gentleman. Let's test your obedience and chivalry. I command you to finish making my breakfast, while I shower and change clothes."

Alex tilts his toward the clothes he selected for her.

"Oh, I set out an outfit for you. But, I don't know what church leaders wear. Or, any woman for that matter."

Christina glances over at the outfit and giggles. "A dress under my priestly robes?! Uuummm, I'm not tryin' to bed … our father!" She laughs uproariously.

Alex chuckles and wipes sweat from his brow. "Whew! The way you worded that made it sound uber creepy and incestual!"

Christina giggles and gets outta bed. Alex heads to the kitchen. Christina hurries to remove her blouse, before Alex leaves the room. She's hoping Alex catches a glimpse! The fact that there's no reaction gravely disappoints her.

Alex reemerges in the kitchen, where he busies himself completing Christina's breakfast. He finds some leftover asparagus. He grabs a banana and some lemon wedges. He finds some slices of honey ham.

Alex debates about whether to attribute any of Christina's doings to God.

"Oh, well. Why not? Thank God she's so nutrition conscious! Now, back to the omelet."

Alex continues cooking. He reheats the asparagus and adds ham, tomatoes, cheese, salt, pepper, a tad of milk and eggs to the omelet mixture. When the egg mixture in a pan is on the stove, Christina comes forth from her room.

Alex offers: "if you need some extra energy, you might wanna put a slice of bread or two in the toaster."

Christina: "It couldn't hurt. Right?"

She grabs two slices of whole wheat bread to place in the toaster.

Christina looks at all the assorted foods on the counter: "How did you find all these random ingredients?"

Alex: "I have my ways."

Christina laughs long and loud.

Alex sniffles and fakes wiping a tear. "Ya know what hurts the most? It's the lack of respect!"

The two sit at the kitchen table.

Alex: "Now, lemme explain each of these ingredients:

First off, obviously, there are eggs, which contain almost every nutrient we need. They're rich in HDL—the good cholesterol. Eggs have loads of cysteine—an amino acid that breaks down toxins. Ethyl alcohol is a toxin. The next ingredient is the ham, a terrific source of protein, iron and potassium. Next up are the tomatoes. They contain carotenoids to help vision. Asparagus contains inulin, which improves digestion. Plus, asparagus has many enzymes that break down alcohol. So, whenever you drink a lot—like last night—eat some asparagus to combat the hangover."

Christina's eyes widen. "How do you know all this?"

Alex: "I've always been a curious nerd as to what goes in my body. Speaking of 'going in the body'." He smiles and winks at Christina. "The asparagus root—famously known as shatavari—is excellent for helping with fertility. Finally, bananas are high in potassium, which strengthens muscles and relaxes the brain, lowering blood pressure."

Christina tosses aside her napkin, reaches across the table, grabs Alex by his shirt collar and pulls him in for a looong, wet kiss.

Afterwards, Alex stammers: "Certainly not that I'm complainin'! But, what'd I do?!"

Christina again grabs his collar to look him eye to eye.

"Didn't you get the memo? Smart is the new sexy."

She yanks in his face for lip lock round two.

NEW SERVICE

As surprised and excited as Alex is about Christina's affection, he realizes what he must do. He stays over to monitor Christina's good health, which includes her safe travel to work.

Alex: "You okay to drive?"

Christina: "Uuummm, … yeah."

She fakes stumbling over a chair, before she actually stubs a toe while trying to catch herself.

"Ooowwwzzzaaa! Son of a … gun!"

Alex: "Jeez. Your eye-foot coordination seems to be a bit off." He chuckles. How 'bout I drive you there?"

Christina fakes uncertainty. "Uuummm, … yeah. I'd appreciate that. Would you please stay for the service?"

Alex: "Church really isn't my thing. But, for you, …" Heavy audible sigh. "I'll sack it up."

Christina giggles.

"How would someone sack it down? Could a girl sack it in any direction?"

They take Alex's car to Christina's church. After a short drive, they pull into the church parking lot. This church is ginormous. Christina directs Alex where to go and where she'll sit.

Christina: "There's another service at eleven. But, I'll spare you from a second one. I'll just say I've got a stomachache."

Alex asks: "What'd you eat? Is it the flu? Sports injury?" He chuckles. "Swine flu?"

Christina: "What? Why?"

Alex: "Details! The best lies leave no options or possibilities."

Christina: "Ugh. Fine! I'll just say it's…" Air quotes. "… lady problems."

Alex: "Eeeewwww!"

There is an awkward silence.

Christina: "Exactly the reaction I'm goin' for—repulsion with zero follow up questions."

Alex: "Ha ha ha. I appreciate the sympathy. So, what would you like to do, while you play hooky?"

As Christina slowly walks away, she says, "You'll hafta wait and seeeee."

She deliberately forces Alex to sit through the entire service—in suspense, before he knows what's next. Alex recognizes her scheming, but it's too late to complain.

He grins over his being outfoxxed. "That little she-devil outsmarted me! Well, propz to her. The end justifies the means."

Oh, Sweet Irony

The topic of the church service on this day is the various reasons for leaving the church, and which excuses God considers legitimate. Throughout the sermon, Alex is loudly sighing, rolling his eyes and miming blowing his brain out. In doing so, he even causes a few nearby attendants to laugh. One guy snorted.

After the sermon, Alex's relieved to find Christina.

Alex: "You displayed remarkable aplomb during the sermon! I really liked that. Would you mind, if I said you were astonishingly attractive just sitting there listening to the priest's words? And, while you were passed out sleeping last night?"

Christina's confused.

"But, I didn't speak. I was merely a bystander … like you. Huh? What? Thank you so much!"

Alex: "Sssooooooo, what shall we do? The suspense is killing me!"

Christina: "Well, I really like watching you cook. But, I really wanna hear about your job as a film critic. Would you mind, if I just invited myself over?"

Alex: "And, I talked about movies, while I made us a meal? Not at all! How 'bout some crispy parmesan garlic chicken with zucchini? I looooove this dish! … P.S. Might you wanna bring your swimsuit, … if you wanna go in my pool?"

Christina: "Mmmmm mmm! That sounds absolutely delightful! I'm all in! Including the pool! So, when's this all goin' down? Tonight?"

Alex: "Well, since there's no time regulation on swimming—as long as it's over 20 minutes after eating, wanna start now?"

Christina: "Swim now and eat later? Sure! Should I go home to get my suit?" Christina wantingly eyes Alex, as she asks.

Her playfulness is completely lost on Alex.

"Well, ... yeah. You might need that."

He chuckles awkwardly.

Alex drives to Christina's house.

In her driveway, Christina instructs him: "I'll run in real quick. You just wait here." She runs inside the house. She returns in breakneck speed with a small bag. "I'm ready to go."

While riding, Christina asks: "So, what'd you think of the sermon?"

Alex: "Honestly? I thought that the church seems rather hypocritical, if it eliminates our right to free will. Let's say you have a completely life changing event—good or bad—that totally alters your views on faith and beliefs. Does doctrine really forbid ambivalence?"

Christina: "Hhhmmm. That's a great point. But, I think the father was trying to emphasize that once you've seen the right way, then why leave it?"

Alex: "Does the church not recognize the concept of live and learn? Or, the scientific method?"

Christina giggles. "The church and science don't really get along."

Alex: "'Cuz one is fact based, while the other is all hearsay, opinions and conjecture?"

Christina rolls her eyes and giggles, as they pull into Alex's driveway. The two enter Alex's abode.

Alex: "Swimming?"

Alex walks into his bedroom to change into his swimwear. Christina enters the bathroom to do the same. After a few minutes, Alex emerges and calls out: "Christina! How's it goin'?!"

Christina's response: "Well, I think I'm fine. But, you tell me ..."

She emerges ssslllooooowwwlllyyy from the bathroom. Buck naked.

Alex's excitedly surprised to behold such a beauty. He quickly shuts his eyes and puts up his hand to be polite.

Alex chuckles and stutters: "Uuum, ha ha ha. Are we f fuh for forgetting something?"

Christina: "Uuum, no. I'm more comfortable like this. Care to join me in the pool?"

Alex giggles like an excited schoolgirl and replies: "Ask, and you shall receive."

He pantses himself and runs to the pool.

"Race ya!"

The two have tons o' fun in the water. Hugs and kisses and just 'cuz Alex's obsessed with quality health, forty pool length laps. Christina only completes twenty laps. She just watches Alex swim. She shivers.

Christina asks, "Why is it so cold?!"

Alex explains: "Well, I keep the water cold to instigate more exercise. Ya see, the colder temperature forces the muscles to expand and contract at a greater rate to generate more body heat, thereby expending more calories."

He glances at Christina and adds: "Your constricted capillaries indicate that the water's a bit chilly."

Christina looks confused.

Alex clarifies. "'Tis a tid bit nipply."

Christina smiles and folds her arms across her chest.

Swim Before Eat

Alex—to Christina: "And now, I fix a late lunch. My gut tells me you're hungry."

Christina: "Well, that's a smart 'gut' you've got there. Why am I so starving?"

Alex: "Well, the constant muscle contractions burn excessive calories. So, your body seeks to replenish its nourishment. On that note, let's eat or, cook some chicken

Alex melts 2 tablespoons of butter in a large skillet over medium high heat. He sets out a few dishes. One for the liquified butter, and the bread crumbs, parmesan cheese and flour mixture in dish number two. Next, he dips a raw chicken breast in dish number one. Then, he coats said breast in dish number two and lays it in the butter coated skillet. He repeats this coating process with five more chicken breasts.

Christina's in awe. "Wowza! Jeez. How do you multitask so well?"

Alex caters to his audience with his instant response: "Idle hands are the devil's playground."

Christina comments: "Wow. A smart, strongman who cooks for me, skinny dips with me, and knows theological principles? You've captured my heart!"

Alex grins big and states: "Geographically, and anatomically, the shortest route to a beautiful woman's heart is through her stomach."

Alex grins and cooks the opposite side of each chicken breast for another four minutes each so, the outside is crispy. He sets the six chicken breasts aside in dish number three for future use. He adds two more tablespoons of butter and some minced garlic to the skillet. During the minute or so of their sautéing, Alex quickly slices two large zucchini. In turn, Alex adds the zucchini, a pinch of salt and pepper and about two tablespoons of parmesan cheese. He re adds the chicken breasts and heats 'em for a minute or two.

Alex: "Christina, wanna bring over your plate?"

Christina: "Wow, Alex. That looks mouthwatering. Literally."

Alex serves each of them two chicken breasts with zucchini slices. The couple sit for grace and dining on the pool patio.

Christina emphatically thanks God for "blessing her with such a generous and intelligent hunk, who methodically cooks up a storm!" And then in a hushed voice: "Plus, some … other stuff."

Christina: "Mmm mmm mmm mmmmmmm! The zucchini's a great touch!"

Alex: "Want some toast or a roll? Carbs are energy."

Christina: "No, thanks. This is delicious, as is!"

Alex: "So, gorgeous. Hhhwhat would you like to discuss?"

Christina: "First of all, please do not start the h thing again. Next, tell me about your job."

Alex: "Well, I'm a film critic. I actually get paid to watch movies!" He kinda half snickers.

"Usually three to four per day. And, I write an extensive critique of each. I've got a convenient, connection at the local movie theater. Staff wants positive advertising for their establishment. Sooooo, they treat me to free concessions and private viewings. My work hours are flexible. But, my weekday is usually about 9:00 am to 5:00 pm. As a result, I've seen countless films."

Christina: "Nice date conversation. It obviously works."

She winks and smiles at him. "What about recreation? Like, what do you do … for fun?

Alex: "Well, I train in and teach kids' martial arts—karate and jujitsu. Plus, I think of clever compliments. You brag about your indefatigable beauty—as you rightly should. Are you still considered…" Air quotes. "Full o' yourself, if you're merely stating facts?"

Christina: "Oh, yeah! When can I come in to watch a class?"

Alex: "Tuesdays and Thursdays. Early evening. Saturday mornings you're kinda busy. So, during the week, just come here. We'll go together."

Christina: "Alright. So, Tuesday. Yay!"

Alex: "Just recently, I met up with an ol' buddy, who introduced me to his wife, Lisa. As I've been really struggling in the dating realm, she volunteered to set me up with some *encounters* with single ladies."

"What, what? Other single ladies? Do I mean nothing to you?" Christina's distraught.

"Am I just another notch on your bedpost?!"

Alex: "Excuuuse me? We haven't even made love!"

Christina: "Oh, yeah? What about that night that you got me so drunk, that I passed out, and you slept with me in my bed to make me your little succubus?"

Alex: "First off, you poured yourself those three additional glasses of wine. Secondly, I stayed over just to make sure you'd be safe throughout the night. We only snuggled! Finally, what's a 'succubus'?"

Christina: "Okay, Poindexter. I'da thought that your amazing intelligence would know that my petite bodily frame cannot handle that much liquor. And, your intimidating physical body could've stopped me, if you wanted to. Also, a 'succubus' is a female demon believed to have sexual intercourse with sleeping men."

Alex looks horrified. He gathers himself and calmly retorts:

"Responsible alcohol imbibing is not just about one's anatomic build. It also factors in drinking speed, accompanying food and drink inhalation and imbibing frequency. You drank nothing else but four glasses of zinfandel in about twenty minutes. Are you singin' the ol' school nirvana song, *Rape Me?* If so, then no way! Finally, there's no way I would or could ever sleep through sexual intercourse with a beauty such as yourself."

Christina exhales a deep, audible sigh of relief: "Wheeewww!"

Alex: "C'mooon! Did you seriously think that I would rape you? Not a chance in heh … unexplored Antarctica!"

Christina giggles. "Thank you for your comforting analogy. And, my whole argument was just a trick to get you to admit a few romantic things you've done for me, and say what was motivating you. Now, I'm 100% positive you have a genuine heart. You've really made me rethink many issues. Thanks, babe."

Misunderstanding Resolved

Alex's pleasantly surprised at Christina's affectionate reference to him.

Alex excitedly asks her: "Are we devising pet names for each other now?"

Christina: "Well, my 'babe' was pretty much off the cuff. So, I'm thinking, soon. Sure."

Alex clears the table and brings the dirty plates to the dishwasher in the kitchen. As he's exiting the kitchen, Christina confronts him at the patio door, moans, "Come here, stud," and wraps her arms around his burly chest. Almost inexplicably, Alex pulls his mouth away and says,

"Jeez. I was gonna offer you dessert! But, …" he shrugs.

Christina counters: "You're my dessert!"

Christina hops up to hug Alex. He catches her under her hamstrings. So, now he's supporting her about four feet off the floor with her arms' hugging him and her tongue's cascading around the deluge of her saliva that is in Alex's mouth.

Still holding her up, Alex motions toward the patio. But, Christina digs her heels into Alex's floating ribs and midsection, as if he's her race horse.

"Whoa! Brake, boy. Turn toward the bedroom." She lightly kicks his lower abdomen as a signal to speed up.

Alex warns her: "Careful of my groin, sweetheart. Precious cargo!"

Utterly bewildered by Christina's desired destination, Alex just goes along with his jockey's commands. When Alex pulls up outside his bedroom door, he pauses.

He can feel Christina's bodyweight's shifting on his back. With her free hands, Christina nudges open the bedroom door. Alex can feel her squirming away, trying to get loose.

So, he just yells, "bombs away," and drops her legs. He turns to face her, and his jaw nearly hits the ground. Christina has somehow managed to wiggle out of her blouse. So, she just stands there in the hallway, wearing only a hearts-decorated brassiere and cargo pants. She looks very business-ready from the waist down.

Alex: "Pardon my effrontery. But, what the heck are you thinkin'?"

He chuckles and rushes to put his hands over his crotch, as a true joke.

Christina shyly lifts her hands up to attempt to hide a portion of her billowing chest. To no avail.

Alex: "Wouldn't any lustful activities we indulge in be considered 'sinful' and forbidden in the eyes of the church? For some ridiculous and outdated reason?"

Christina sighs deeply. "What, you don't like? You're right. I'm sorry."

She reaches to pick up her balled-up blouse from the floor.

Alex firmly interjects: "Not like? I said nothing of the sort! I am both aghast and lightheaded, as approximately 5.6 liters of blood is all rushing to my groin."

Christina looks confused at first. After a minute or two of processing, she broadly smiles and body checks Alex into his room. She closes the door behind her.

"So, Alex, gimme your best lines."

Alex: "'Lines'? Like pre-arranged, cookie cut sayings to promote romantic excitement? I have none of those. I'm damn proud, that I alter my speech per my audience. For you, I know that you live by the Book, which is why I'm completely perplexed as to what has gotten into you!"

Christina: "Oddly, that unapologetic honesty works on me! And, the church has been indecisive for years regarding whether priests are permitted to have sex. My stance is if there's no definitive papal doctrine specifically against it, then why not?"

Alex: "Ha ha! When in Rome, right?"

Christina: "Actually, it'd be 'when not in … about 6.1 miles … from Rome, do as the Romans do.'"

Alex: "Really? Then, that means … Vatican City is … approximately 9.82 kilometers from Rome, as the locals would say. Since Europeans are smart enough to use the metric system."

Christina: "Wow. Jeez!" She leaps—bare chested—up into Alex's arms and bombards him with kisses. "Your intelligence just relaxes—yet excites me."

Alex: "Well, your excitement really stimulates my excitement, … as you can probably feel. But, I'd be more relaxed, if you could explain your sudden change of heart regarding your moral responsibility to the sexual specifics of the church."

Christina: "Well, today's service got me thinking—do I trust the logic of my brain, the continuity of my faith, or the desires of my heart?"

Alex scratches his head and makes a face, as if he's deep in thought.

"Hhhmmm, that's quite a predicament. Maybe you need some time to weigh your options?"

Christina: "Aw, shucks. I suppose you're right, though."

She picks up her blouse and puts it back on her torso.

Alex: "Should I take you home?"

Christina sighs audibly. "Would you please? I'll let you know my thoughts on Tuesday, when I come watch your kids' jujitsu class."

FOR THE KIDS

Alex just kinda goes through the motions of his next two days at work. Four movie viewings with four movie critiques followed by three films with three critiques. As per his routine on Tuesdays and Thursdays, he makes sure to leave right at five, so he can make any last-minute teaching notes before class. In this particular instance, he changes the theme of Tuesday's lesson to Takedowns to Mount Control. He just hopes Christina's there to see it and put two and two together.

In class Alex emphasizes the similarities between the evening's lesson and folk style wrestling. He aims to prepare his students for amateur wrestling in high school.

Alex to students: "Maybe even college wrestling too, for all you smart kids with tenacity. So, I'm lookin' at you, Jeffrey." Alex pauses and chuckles. "Naw. Any of you, kids, has the smarts to wrestle well. You've just gotta be tenacious and improvisational."

Kid student raises his hand and asks: "But, what would our names be—like 'Ultimate Warrior'? 'Cuz, Sensei Alex, sir, would you be my 'Big Boss Man'?"

Alex: "No, silly. That's professional wrestling! Wrestling entertainment, as they call it. There's a ginormous difference. I mean, I'll support you, no question. I just don't like that fake crud. Sooooo, let's examine our interpretation."

Just in time, Christina enters the dojo and quietly sits down in a chair in the back. Alex notices her sleuth-like arrival.

"Class, before we begin, I'd like to bring all your attention to the lovely lady in the back. Christina Jones is the children's pastor at the Missions of Jesus Followers church in nearby Pembroke Pines. She's interested in helping to shape your growing faith and beliefs."

Christina blushes, smiles, and curtsies.

Alex: "But, boys. Hands off! Especially you, Jacob! She has cooties, and only I have the self-defense know how to handle her oddities. But, if you'd like to shape your faith, please speak with her."

Three students turn toward Christina.

Alex to class: "After class. Now, let's scheme how to get to the ground."

Alex reads each explanation—before each move—to the class, as he and a student perform each step.

Technique #1:

It's an arm swing takedown to *juji gatame*.

Attacker and defender face each other.
1. Attacker thrusts a right-handed hook punch at defender's left midsection. He pauses to allow time for he and a sempai—assistant teacher—to perform each move.
1) Defender steps forward right with own right leg and executes a left-handed *shuto uke* to block strike.
2) Defender steps—with own right leg—toward attacker's blocked right arm.
3) Defender thrusts own right arm over/outside of attacker's right arm and down toward the ground and presses own chest against attacker's right arm as a counterbalance.
4) Defender rotates own torso counterclockwise (toward own left), as defender sandwiches attacker's right arm between own right bicep and chest.
5) Defender shifts own right leg back against attacker's right leg,

as defender leans forward/down and rotates own trunk counterclockwise (to own left) to take down attacker.
6) On ground, defender slides own left leg over attacker's neck ... with attacker's right arm trapped between defender's legs.
7) Defender—while lying on own back— thrusts own hips upward, while pushing own legs together—against attacker's right elbow and pulling attacker's right wrist down—toward own chest."

Alex: "Great job, kids! Who's gonna use that one?" All the students' hands shoot up. "Any questions?" Billy slowly raises his hand. "What's a *juji gatame*?"

Alex: "Weren't you watching, Billy? Come here."

Billy: "No. Of course I was watching! I mean the English translation of *juji gatame*.

Alex: "Oooh! A *juji gatame* is a cross body armlock. It's actually the most popular armlock in the world. It's definitely my favorite. So, if anyone wants bonus points on their advancement test, ..."

He motions his head downward toward the floor.

"Now, next up! I call it the Fireman's Carry to Juji."

Attacker and defender stand and face each other.
1) Attacker steps with right leg toward defender and executes a right-handed *mawashi zuki* or roundhouse punch.
2) Defender steps forward and right with own right leg and executes an extended left-handed *shuto uke* to attacker's right wrist.
3) Defender quickly pops a right-handed vertical *uraken*— or backfist—to attacker's bridge of nose.
4) Defender drops into a fireman prep by grabbing attacker's right elbow, rotating/raising it, shooting in with own right leg and thrusting own right arm between attacker's legs and up toward attacker's

back/head/shoulders.
5) Attacker tries to sprawl back. But, the weight shift actually tightens defender's grip.
6) Defender pulls attacker's right arm down with own left hand while thrusting own right arm up—between attacker's legs and toward attacker's back.
7) Defender bends toward own left, pulling attacker's upper body down over defender's shoulders.
8) Immediately after attacker falls, defender—still holding attacker's right arm—swings own left leg over attacker's head/neck on the ground.
9) Defender leans back—while pulling attacker's right arm with own body lean.
10) Defender pushes/pulls own hips/knees/legs together—against attacker's arm/elbow.
11) Defender finishes by heel kicking attacker's face with own left foot."

Sensei Alex—to class: "Remember—yes, this stomp is a finishing move. But, there's no reason to be so emphatic that you put your guard down. It's more about placement than power. You stomp the ankle to prevent more threatening chasing. Correctly channeled aggression can overcome some flaws."

Alex: "Way to be, kids! Let's take a water break. I hafta talk to Ms. Jones. Then, we'll continue."

The kids all get up, run to the door, bow out, and run to the water fountain.

Alex—privately to Christina: "So, what do ya think?"

Christina: "Wow, I really love it! Plus, it's yet another skill you have. You are so sexy, when you're…" Air quotes. "In your element, whether it's cooking meals or swimming laps or solving math or evaluating movies or teaching martial arts or hangin' with kids."

Alex: "Sooooo, you are gonna recommend my dojo to your kids?"

Christina: "Uuummm, … duh! Shooooot, I wanna return myself!"

Alex: "Well, I still attend class at a different dojo to learn from higher ranking black belts than myself a few times a week. You could be my training partner."

Christina: "That'd be alotta fun. When's class?"

Alex: "Mondays, Wednesdays, Saturdays and Sundays. …"

Alex: "Actually, never mind. Those are black-belts-only workouts. How 'bout some many private lessons?"

Christina: "Ooooooo! Even better! Where and when might these be?"

Alex: "At my house! Whenever you want!"

He laughs hard and winks at Christina.

Christina: "Well, thanks, Alex. You're really being my Prince Charming!"

After the *karateka* return, Sensei Alex teaches another technique and monitors grappling sessions. After class, most of the *karateka* run to talk to Christina. Alex grabs her for an aside. "These kids are very visually stimulated. So, be pretty. Be pretty!"

Christina—faux offended—giggles and retorts: "Are you implying that—usually—I'm not?"

Alex laughs loudly and walks away, as he signals to the kids to approach Christina.

Gotta Talk It Out

When her informative talks with the martial arts students finish, Christina finds Alex to clear up some confusion.

Christina: "That was a fabulous class! I love how you give the students so much independence to kinda teach themselves. You act as more of an enlightened guide. That's a fabulous teaching technique."

Alex: "Exactly! I will only do so much. Who knows you better than you?"

Christina: "Well, you know 'em pretty well! Tangent: I cannot get these 'other women' outta my head! So, are you using my friend, Lisa, as your female pimp? Are you in some kind of dating service?!"

Alex: "Heavens no! I was merely frustrated with my lack of success on the dating front. Ya see, you indirectly and unintentionally taught me life chess. In the game of chess that is life, there are kings, and there are pawns."

He tightly clasps her hand and pulls her face close to his.

"Then, I met you. Previous ladies were all merely pawns. You appear to be my king … gender aside."

Alex lightly pushes the back of her head closer to his, as he leans forward to wet her lips with his.

At this point, some students have reentered the dojo and are loudly whispering and snickering, as they wait for their parents in the back.

Billy: "Sensei Alex, I thought you warned us that Ms. Christina has cooties and that we shouldn't kiss her."

Jacob: "Or, we hafta do alotta pushups!"

Alex glances at Christina. She very cutely smiles then shrugs.

Alex to Jacob: "I did say that."

He lies prostrate on the floor.

Alex asks the onlookers: "How many?"

Billy: "Uuuummm, … fifty!"

Jacob: "No, a hundred!"

Alex sighs. He glances up at Christina. She shrugs and mouths, "I'm sorry."

Alex raises up on his knuckles and starts the punishment. Sensei Alex's still teaching. Down then up: "Notice that I lower myself slowly, 'cuz that forces the muscles to control the descent. But, then I spring up quickly for that burst."

Jacob's in awe. "On his knuckles? Jeeeeez."

Alex: "Well, thirty-six years of training will give you, at least, a small degree of muscle memory."

Alex completes all 100 pushups and waves goodbye to the kids. After they've all been picked up, Alex's alone with Christina.

Alex: "Sooooo, what now?"

Christina: "Well, wow. I didn't think you could impress me more. But, after watching you teach, I was wrong. Hhhmmm. What time is it?"

Alex glances up at the clock. "Uuummm. It's about …"

Christina: "Who cares? Ya mind if I come over?"

Alex excitedly: "Not at all!"

THE JUICE IS WELL WORTH THE SQUEEZE

Alex locks up the dojo and departs for home. Christina follows in her car. When the two arrive, they hug outside, before they enter Alex's domicile.

Alex: "May I get you a drink?"

Christina: "I'll just have a glass of water, thanks."

Alex serves her some cold water.

Christina: "So, in case you haven't put it all together, I weighed your pluses against your minuses."

Alex: "And? … and?"

Christina: "Well, Alex. Your stunning intelligence, flattering charm, comforting respect and commendable treatment of children tipped the scale of my heart in your favor over my theological past. Thus, I'm considering you to be my Mr. Right Now. And, I'm bankin' on your eventually makin' me drop the 'Now'."

Alex: "That's fuckin' interesting. Well, you're my Cinderella."

Christina: "Is it cliché to say that you ultimately won me over tonight after your teaching demonstration, … when you 'sealed it with a kiss'?"

Alex laughs.

"That's not cliché. You're just quoting an old Britney spears song."

Christina giggles.

"How ironic! When we were standing together at your dojo, with all the kids around, I wanted to quote another Britney song to you, 'If we could escape the crowd somehow? If I said I want your body now? Would you hold it against me?'… Well, would you?"

Alex without any hesitation: "I certainly, undoubtedly would! Just, how can I be positive that this is what you want? I do not want to mess with your faith."

Christina: "Reeelax, hun! Didn't you hear me? … You won!"

Alex: "Well, only if you insist! Do you hafta be anywhere in the morning?"

Christina smiles coyly.

"Only in your arms."

Alex: "Aaawww. Aren't you …? A sweet, adorable, little kitten? So, you don't have work or anything? On a Wednesday?"

Christina: "Have you already forgotten what I do, Alex? I'm a children's pastor. I only work the weekends."

Alex: "Just that? Are you alright, money wise?"

Christina: "My wealthy father passed away eight years ago. So, I got a pretty sizable inheritance. That allows me to work two days a week. Listen, your very existence has captivated me! From movies to cooking to teaching to generosity to smarts. I'm just mesmerized. Sooooo, may I pleeease sleep here tonight?"

Alex: "Aaaaalright. But, just 'cuz you're ridiculously beautiful! Okay?"

Alex mimes panicking. He has his arms' sticking straight out in front of him and his eyes shut. "Where'd you go? I got lost in your eyes."

Christina giggles.

"Jeeeez! I hope you don't have white sheets. 'Cuz if you say a cheesy line like that tonight, I'm gonna barf."

Alex gets sheets and a pillow for the living room couch. Christina's very confused. She exclaims, quizzingly: "What—on Earth—are you doing? Do you like to build forts like you're eight years old?"

Alex: "Well, I just figured that you'd sleep in my bed, and I'd sleep out here."

Christina cackles from just outside Alex's bedroom doorway. "Well, you thought wrong! Come here!"

Show Appreciation

Alex hobbles over like Igor Dr. Frankenstein's hunchbacked assistant of. Alex stumbles in on Christina, grinning in the middle of his bedroom. Alex explains his injury: "Little Eric accidentally stepped on my ankle, while I was demonstrating in class today. It's just a minor handicap. Actually…" He straightens his posture. "It's more of a leg-icap."

Christina grins.

She asks: "Do you have any romantic music?"

Alex: "To set the mood?"

Inexperienced and confused, Christina replies: "Uuuuummm. What do you mean?"

Alex chuckles upon realizing just how little Christina knows. "Exactly how much of a love neophyte are you?"

Christina interprets "neophyte" as a religious nonbeliever. So, she's almost offended.

"Need I remind you what my job's been for the last … twelve years? Of course, I'm not a neophyte!"

Alex's unaware of the "neophyte" religious meaning of a heathen or heretic. So, he merely smiles and nods.

Christina worriedly—but innocently—asks: "Don't you need music to better establish some kind of rhythm?"

Alex's internally freakin' out, 'cuz he doesn't like music! He's more visual, like his students. Soon, however, he devises a plan.

"You want a relaxing pace? I just always seeeee numbers. So, how 'bout I recite random math trivia, while you lie there and not fall asleep from boredom? 'Cuz, didn't you say that my math knowledge is sexy?"

Christina giggles nervously.

"I did say that, didn't I? 'cuz it is." Deep, inhalation and audible exhalation, "Oh, well. Why not?"

Alex saunters over to gently grab Christina, to slowly kiss her lips and neck and to maneuver his hands to the back of her blouse. Christina steps away. She says: "Fast forward."

She proceeds to remove her precautionary raincoat, slip off her blouse, do away with her brassiere and hop into Alex's bed.

Alex excitedly: "FYI. For next time… Let me work to get you in bed. The anticipation only heightens the impending pleasure."

The two begin their coitus. After about four minutes and countless compliments, Alex starts reciting random math mumbo jumbo. "The sum of the first hundred prime numbers is 1111, … which is numerically palindromic. There are 40,320—or 8 factorial—minutes in four weeks.

22273 is the largest prime in the Bible, and it's aptly in numbers 3:43."

Christina lets loose a banshee like scream of glee! The two rest momentarily to gather their thoughts. Christina explains, "That's what did it. The combination of math and a biblical verse … coming out of your mouth." She signs.

The two snuggle and watch TV from bed awhile. When Alex feels himself start to nod off, he leans over to a wide awake Christina and innocently inquires, "Round two now? Or, in the morning?"

She grabs his broad shoulders and pulls his chest onto hers. "How much math you got left?"

Alex slyly smiles big, chuckles and replies, "Don't tempt me."

So, the two engage in another act of love making. Again, Alex's got round upon round of numeric ammo.

"169 is equal to 13 squared. And, its reverse—961—is equal to 31 squared. 122 multiplied by 213 = 25986. Interestingly, if you reverse 122 and 213, their product would also be the reverse of 25986. In other words, 221 × 312 = 68952."

He continues, "I got bored…." Awkward pause). "When I worked as a cashier! Not with you! So, I played with the coins. It turns out, … there are 292 … no, 293 … ways to make change for a dollar bill by using pennies, nickels, dimes, quarters and half dollars. The symbol for division is called an obelus. On the other hand, the division slash (/) is called a virgule.

I believe 'tis Psalms chapter 90, verse … um … 12 that states: 'So teach [us] to number our days, that we may apply [our] hearts unto wisdom.'"

Christina, again, unleashes her triumphant scream of happiness and satisfaction. The two chat and snuggle for a while.

Christina: "How do you do all that you do? Teaching martial arts, critiquing movies, maintaining a lovely home, keeping in great physical shape, knowing tons of math trivia, memorizing biblical verses and dazzling a peculiar girlfriend?"

Alex: "'Girlfriend?! Whoa! New … and welcome shit has certainly sprung forth. I didn't realize that we'd reached that momentous level of intimacy! My little angel!"

Christina: "Well, what else would you consider me to you?! I'm certainly not Mary Magdalene!"

Alex: "Right now, you're behaving as my personal Christ, 'cuz you're savin' me from a life of solitude and loneliness … and hopelessness. Thanks be to you!"

Alex leans over and kisses Christina's forehead.

"Is it blasphemous to call you my Cryst-eena?"

Christina: "Your 'Krie steena'?" She giggles. "'Tis a little blasphemous, yes. But, if you say it to just me … in private, … it's kind

of a turn on."
　　Alex: "Hhhmmm. Good to know."
　　Christina: "On that note, good night, sweet prince."
　　She lunges forward and kisses him on the lips.

Two Peas in a Pod

The following morning Alex gets up very early. His clock alarm also awoke Christina … at 6:15 AM. He showers quickly and gets ready for work.

Christina: "Now, ya mind if I shower real quick?"

At first, she kicks herself for going against her long-possessed beliefs against sexual desire. Thus, should she try to savagely scrub off her sinful lust? Then, Christina figured that she was not at fault, 'cuz what the heart wants, the heart waaanttts! So, why fight it? She wanted to sneak up on Alex in the shower! But, seeing as Alex's out, Christina makes a pouty face, when she realizes that that ship has sailed.

Christina throws a minor conniption when she exits the shower and realizes she's without clean clothes. She calls out to Alex, "Hey, stud muffin! Can I borrow some clothes?"

Alex: "Sure. Shirts in the closet. Shorts in a drawer."

Christina spends entirely too long picking out an outfit. Finally, about eighteen minutes later, she walks out to a waiting Alex. She picks the pants out of her butt-crack.

Alex laughs. "I'm terribly sorry. Were my thongs not your size?"

Christina joins Alex for a lite breakfast. Open faced Egg McMuffins with sliced ham, cheddar cheese, and sliced hard-boiled egg on an English muffin. And orange juice.

Alex: "How pathetic is it, if I said that last night was heavenly?"

Christina smiles. "It's only pathetic, if I disagree."

There is some silence.

Alex asks Christina to come to his martial arts class on Thursday evening. She agrees. They kiss and head to their respective cars. Alex assures her he'll call.

Since it's Wednesday, Alex has four films to critique today. Busy day. So, he does not shoot the proverbial shit as much with Peter Simmons today. Plus, Alex's smartass comment kinda shuts him up for a while.

Simmons: "Hey, Alex! Wassup, dude? Haven't heard from you in like … a week. Whacha been doin'?"

Alex's sortin' through a mess of paperwork that was mislabeled and misplaced on his desk.

"I've been kinda out of it the last few days. I've been busy with … personal affairs. Plus, I'm tryin' to overcome others' mistakes."

Simmons isn't sure if Alex's referring to Peter's errors or his own. So, he just smiles and nods.

Alex sighs deeply and loudly. "Above all, you must never downplay the extensiveness of stupidity."

Simmons puts his hands up to shoulder level and slowly backs away.

"I'll just leave you alone right now."

Alex plows through his four films that day. Typical Wednesday. But, just to assure Peter Simmons that he—Alex—is just fine, he sneaks up behind the dude to tell him in a loud voice, so much of the office can hear: "Special delivery! For the best big brother ever! Happy hump day!"

Just as Alex recites the last line, he delivers a strong pelvic thrust to Simmons's lower back.

Simmons chuckles but angrily turns toward Alex "One. What's a 'pelvic thrust'? Two. I'm an only child! Three. When did Mr. Depression turn into Mr. Asshole?"

Alex: "One. It's a wrestling move. Two. They don't know that. Three. I've gotta give the people what they want!"

Alex can't put his finger on why. But he is unusually jovial today. He ponders his diet. He ponders his martial arts teachings. He ponders his exercise regimen. He deliberates …

"Eureka!" Alex pops up from his desk chair.

He remembers that he just ended his … sex drought of, like, 9 frickin' years. No wonder he's ecstatic! Actually, Alex was so distraught, … yet eccentric, that he kept a count of his misery: 'Twas ~110.58 months … or ~64.73 weeks … or exactly 3,366 days. But, no more! … Yay!

So, Alex enjoys his typical Wednesday workday and heads home to relax. As he sits at a red light, he admires a giant photo of a young woman lounging on a beach towel at the beach.

He internally compliments the photo: "Wow! Great figure."

Just then, he remembers Christina.

"Oh, yeeeeeaaahhh! I'll call her and invite her over for a swim."

So, when he gets home, he calls Christina.[18] While she contemplated her visiting, Alex congratulated himself for looking past her religious commitments to enjoy her spectacular personality … and phenomenal aesthetic appeal!

He tells himself: "I'll bring that up to her tonight."

Alex over the phone: "And, bring a loose change of clothes, if you want your first private jujitsu class tonight."

Christina excitedly: "Sounds great!"

Alex: "And, if you hurry, you could help me fix dinner."

Hearing that intriguing offer, Christina matter of factly declares: "Aaaaaand, my schedule's clear. I'll leave in ten."

Alex: "Groovy tunes!" Alex gets together a bunch of food for a big dinner.

"Hhhmmm. Red peppers. Green peppers. … a few yellow peppers. Peas. Leftover chicken broth. Noice! Uuuuummm. I'll let Christina

---

[18] Despite owning and possessing a cellular phone, Alex knows the potential dangers of operating said phone while driving.

decide."

From the food items he already has, Alex happily decides on his Thai red curry recipe. Christina can pick either shrimp or chicken. Alex also gets his martial arts notebook to try teaching her some techniques.

The doorbell rings. Alex's surprised that Christina's already there.

"Wow. You certainly made great time! How 'bout we have our workout before our dinner?"

Christina replies in her tank top and sweatpants: "Hhhmmm. Work up our appetites? That's prolly a smart move."

Alex: "Just, you want shrimp or chicken with your curry?"

Christina: "Oh, yeeeaaah! You can cook. Hhhmmm. Can I have both?"

Alex: "Hhhmmm. If you help me, then why not? Now. For you to experience the full teacher effect from me, you must refer to me as Sensei Alex. And, please bow at the door every time you enter or exit the gym area."

The two walk to Alex's exercise room. Alex asks: "From now on, are you okay with my testing out some o' my new techniques on you, before I teach 'em to the kids? Then, you could be one of my sempai's, which are my 'assistant teacher's."

Christina excitedly: "Sure, Alex! I'd looove to help you!"

Alex serious: "Excuuuse you, 'karateka'. I'm Sensei Alex during our workouts. You're gonna learn a 'lil Japanese in your workouts. Otherwise, it's ten pushups each time."

Christina: "Sorry, Alex."

Alex frowns.

Christina: "Anything you want, Sensei Alex."

Alex: "So, I'll just read my description, and show you each technique slowly. Then, we'll make dinner. K? … k. First up, I labeled it, 'arm swing takedown to *juji*."

Attacker and defender face each other.

1) Attacker thrusts a right-handed hook punch at defender's left

midsection."

Christina: "'Hook punch to midsection? Am I doin' this right? Sensei Alex?"

Alex: "Well, my midsection is more in the middle of my body. ... hence the name. You're a' lil low. ... that's my groin!"

Christina: "I'm not seein' a problem."

Alex: ... "So, 2) defender steps forward with her right foot and executes a left handed *shuto uke*—'knife hand block'—to block strike.

3) Defender steps—with own right leg—toward attacker's blocked right arm.

4) Defender thrusts own right arm over and outside of attacker's right arm and down toward the ground and presses own chest against attacker's right arm as a counterbalance.

5) Defender rotates own torso counterclockwise (toward own left), as defender sandwiches attacker's right arm between own right bicep and chest."

Alex Rests his right forefinger on the top of Christina's head, as she spins, like they're dancing.

6) defender shifts own right leg back against attacker's right leg, as defender leans forward /down and rotates own trunk counterclockwise (to own left) to take down attacker.

7) On ground, defender slides own left leg over attacker's neck ... with attacker's right arm trapped between defender's legs."

8) Defender—while lying on own back— thrusts own hips upward, while pushing own legs together—against attacker's right elbow and pulling attacker's right wrist down—toward own chest."

Sensei Alex: "Spectacular job, *sempai!* Sooo, what'd you think?"

Christina: "Wow. I looove the stuff on the floor!"

Alex: "Well, jujitsu is ground fighting. ... sooooo, now you know. Another technique? We'll only do two tonight. K?"

Christina: "Yes, Sensei Alex."

The two stand up. Sensei Alex mentions that the last finish—the *juji gatame*, or cross arm lock—is considered the most powerful armlock in international competition.

Sensei Alex: "Practicing it with you makes it my new favorite lock to get trapped in."

Christina smiles coyly and bats her eyes. "Sweetie, you're just sayin' that, 'cuz you like your arm between my legs!"

'Sensei' Alex: "That's Sensei Sweetie to you. Please gimme ten pushups."

Christina gets down on her hands and knees and starts her pushups.

Sensei Alex: "No. No. No. No! I teach men not wimpy little giiirls! I mean that metaphorically. Proper pushup position is on your hands and feet! You're gonna build some gunz!"

Christina really struggles. She only completes four.

Sensei Alex tries to motivate her. "I find strong, muscular—to an extent—women ridiculously attractive!"

Christina's revitalized! She hurriedly cranks out six more.

Sensei Alex: "Next technique? We'll only do two. Okay. This one is the Juji Counter to Juji.

Attacker and defender stand and face each other.

1) Simultaneously, attacker steps forward with own right foot, thrusts own right hip into defender's lower midsection and reaches own right arm/ hand outside of defender' left arm ... To grab defender's left hip.

2) Since attacker used no loosening up strikes, defender still has own balance. Defender leans and shuffle steps to own left."

Christina: "What's a 'loosening up strike'?"

Alex: "It's a strike or strikes used to occupy an attacker's attention one way. So, he or she doesn't see another more debilitating strike or kick. For example, when I spar, I like to repeatedly kick low—toward the knees. So, you're lookin' low. Then, I'll snap a backfist to your face. Boo yah!"

3) "Defender counters by simultaneously reaching own right hand to

attacker's right hip and swinging own right leg directly behind attacker's left leg.

4) Defender thrusts own right-handed *mawashi zuki* to attacker's face as loosening up strike.

5) Defender takes down attacker with an *ogoshi*, or hip toss.

6) Defender keeps grasp of attacker's left arm and squats into a *juji gatame*."

Christina: "Great finish! I really followed that easily!" She holds up her right index finger. "I do have one question though."

Alex: "Thanks a lot, babe! And, yes. I will show you and better explain a hip toss later. Don't you worry."

Christina: "How'd you know I was having trouble with that one?"

Alex: "J. Robert Oppenheimer said that, "Genius sees the answer before the question." Plus, I keep an eye on your hips. I am a teacher. Sempai."

Christina: "You are a genius … in more ways than one."

She bats her eyes at Alex and blows him a kiss.

Alex: "Au contraire! True genius is the ability to go from A to D without having to go through B and C. I am an A—clearly." He chuckles. "But, I had to go through countless other ladies … Bs and Cs … to get to my D … a dazzling and dainty deity in distress."

Christina—annoyed—loudly sighs. "Other ladies?"

Alex: "Hey, I had to perfect my romance game for you! You deserve the best!"

Alex: "Now, we eat! You want chicken and fish?"

Christina: "If we can, that'd be great!"

Alex: "Since we're cookin', why the heh … heck not?"

Alex sets Christina up at the stove with an oiled skillet and a dish of leftover chicken broth, a container of cornstarch and a whisk. Alex directs Christina to whisk the broth and cornstarch together in the skillet, 'til he needs 'em.

In a different skillet, Alex heats two teaspoons of vegetable oil, 'til it's shimmering. Just a few minutes. He adds curry paste, coconut milk and brown sugar and mixes 'em in to combine the mix. He calls Christina over to add the assorted peppers herself. He stirs the mixture for around seven minutes. Alex adds a few chicken breasts, and Christina adds a bunch of shrimp. Christina—brilliantly—grabs some rice to cook.

Alex flips and stirs the meat for several minutes, before he and Christina high five,kiss and sit down to a lovely dinner! Christina's so, so, sooooo proud of herself for co-cooking such a fantastic meal, that she vigorously makes out with Alex.

Alex semi audibly mutters to himself: "Well done, Chef Dreamy!"

NUMBERS TALK?

After devouring a splendid dinner, Alex sits down to converse with Christina.

"Some people like words. I'm not sure, if you noticed." He sticks his right index finger in his collar and jokingly tugs it aside. "But, I prefer numbers." He laughs at his own joke.

Christina: "I looooove how you quantify everything!"

Alex's now only thinkin' of Christina's wonderful tendency to sexually apex, when Alex discusses math matters in bed: "As a faux scientist, I'd like to conduct an experiment … on you."

Christina: "Oh, crud! Do I get time to study?!"

Alex: "Okay. Here goes:"

Alex busts out his trusted 73 argument. "Seventy-three is the twenty-first prime number. Its mirror, thirty-seven, is the twelfth and its mirror, twenty-one, is the product of multiplying seven and three. In binary talk, 73 is a numeric palindrome, 1001001, which backwards is 1001001."

Christina: "Ok, let's pretend I don't know what a numeric palindrome is. Explain it, as if I were … five."

Alex: "Well, do you know what a numeric palindrome is?"

She shrugs her shoulders.

Alex: "Hhhmmm. So, are we actually pretending? A numeric palindrome is a number that remains the same when its digits are reversed. For example, a birthday on November 11th, 2011 would read as 11/11/11. Conversely, in the bible, a male's first spoken words were to Eve. He said, "Madam, I am Adam.""

Christina interrupts: "Technically, 'twas, 'Madam, I'm Adam.'"

She smiles and comments sarcastically, "Ever heard of a contraction?" She giggles.

Alex: "Seriously? I'm tryin' to prove a mathematical point here. But, you wanna argue about semantics?" Sarcastically: "Okay. So, if Adam weren't so rushed, he'd have eloooongated the I'm to I am. Which brings me to my next point: 1729 is the smallest number representable as a sum of two cubes … in two different ways. 1729 = 13 + 123 = 93 + 103. Any strange occurrences with 1729?"

Christina starts to peel off the shoulder straps of her tank top. "Is it me, or is it gettin' hot in here?"

Alex stands up and makes a repeated dinging sound. "Ding, ding, ding! And, it's confirmed!"

Christina looks puzzled and a lil' worried.

Alex: "My discussing anything numerical or quantitative … gets you all hot and bothered in a romantic sorta way. Why is that?"

Christina blushes: "I just find you irresistible, when you're…" Air quotes. "In your element, whether it's your discussing martial arts or cooking or personal fitness. But, what really gets my motor runnin' is your mathematical puppetry!"

Alex: "Again … why is that?"

Christina: "I dunno! You're the man of science! You tell me. The heart wants what the heart wants."

Alex leans in for a kiss. "On that note …"

Alex slides his hands behind Christina's back and gently nudges her in for a stronger, deeper, … tighter kiss.

The couple slowly walk, hand in hand, to the bedroom, where they kiss more. Alex excitedly pulls his tongue out and away. "I found a song for you!"

On his laptop, Alex finds the ol' school, classic song by Green River Ordinance, *Endlessly*.

"As you know, I am a more visual person. So, I studied the lyrics, and thought of you. I hope you like it. Remember. This is for you … from me."

He plays the song on his laptop speakers.

After the penultimate line "For you I'll always wait." Christina rolls over on top of Alex and violently feasts on Alex's lips and tongue.

"I love this song! Fantastic find!"

Alex: "These lyrics really make me think … of how much you mean to me. Now, I know it's really tacky. But, as I did not—yet—get a ring. But, this song kinda triggered the determination in me."

He runs over to his desk, writes a note, grabs it and runs back.

Musical Trigger?

Alex gets down on one knee. He clears his throat and says, "Since you've already been my romantic savior, would you please do me the honor of accepting my invitation to being my marital, legally bound savior?"

He presents his note to Christina and puts an imaginary ring on her left hand. The note says:

"I. O. U. Big engagement ring."

Christina smiles huge. Ear to ear, nods her head, tears up, and quotes the song: "For you I'll always waaaaait!"

Alex: "Not endlessly!"

The couple emphatically kiss and make love all night. They keep the *Endlessly* song on repeat throughout the night. In the morning, Christina rolls over to awaken Alex.

She inquires: "Soooooo, *Endlessly* kinda has to be our song now, eh?"

Alex: "Uuum. I don't see how it couldn't. Oooh! I meant to compliment you on how majestic you look, even no, especially while you sleep."

Christina smothers him with kisses.

Christina: "This song really got me thinkin'."

Alex: "About anything in particular?"

Christina: "About ecumenical affairs. Ya see, now theology is my job.

But, your pagan life so intrigues me, that I'm considering altering my career. I am so smitten by you, that I just wanna spend so much time with you. I'm considering becoming ..." She audibly gulps. "A proselyte."

Alex: "Pardon me. But, I have no idea what a proselyte is. But, as long as it's not a man, then I'm cool with your change."

Christina giggles. "A proselyte is a person of changed religious belief. My man is not religious ... in any way. And, I wanna be with him more. So, what if I changed jobs? Would I eventually alter my career?"

Alex: "Well, if you're interested, you could become my main *sempai*. As a part time ... what not."

He glances over at Christina's unhappy face. He inquires, "Aaawww, why are you pouting? What's wrong, sweetie?"

Christina: "I'm not pouting. I'm lamenting. That's the mysteriously sexy way to pout. Don't ya think?"

Alex: "Well, according to me, you always look sexy. But, honestly, you're way sexier, when you're happy ... and smiling."

He wanders around his room to pick up a bead collection and gives it as a gift to Christina.

"Here. These are some 'worry beads' I picked up, when I was abroad in Turkey. Since I'm not religious—nor worrisome, I would like to give my beads to you, ... in hopes that you'll think of your happiness with me and relax."

Christina: "Aaawww! Honey! Jeez, what are these made of?"

Alex: "They're amber."

Christina climbs on top of Alex and kisses him ... looong and wet.

Alex begrudgingly pushes her aside.

He whimpers: "Not now, honey. I have work. Tonight?!"

Christina giggles. "Now, who's givin' the I.O.U.s?"

The two share a quick, lite breakfast before hurrying out in their respective cars. Christina's overjoyed. When she gets home, she calls all of her friends to share her spectacular news.

OTHER COMMITMENTS

At Alex's next kids' martial arts teaching class, then again at his black-belts-only martial arts learning class, Alex's informed of an upcoming United States Martial Arts Leaders Association conference. As a recognized *sensei* and a respected *nidan* and *shodan*, he knows he's gotta go to that meeting.

After that Thursday's martial arts kids' class, Christina comes over to Alex's house, as she's made a custom or habit or tradition. After their shower, Alex mentions the conference.

Christina begs, "Ooooo! May I pleeease accompany you?"

Alex: "Well, it's all the way in Minnesota from South Florida. That's a few hours away ... by plane. I'd much prefer you safe at home. Ya see, according to *The Economist*, the probability of your plane going down is only about one in 5.4 million. But, that means, there's still a chance! And, according to the World Bank's data, only about 95.7% of passengers survive a plane crash. So, you let me, and only me worry about air travel."

Christina admits that she's uber thankful for the proposal and that she's, "already told ... like ... all her friends about it. And, they all wanna come, of course. Sooooooo, can I have a big guest list?"

Alex: "Whatever you want, doll. Just to remind you, I'll be gone this weekend at the conference. Don't miss me too much. But, call me whenever you want!"

Christina: "When you leavin'? Need a ride to the airport?"

Alex: "I leave Friday evening. A buddy from work's gonna give me a ride straight from the office. Hey! As a matter of fact…" He runs to stand directly in front of her. "I'd be honored, Ms. fiancée, if you…" He pulls a house key out of his pocket and hands it to Christina. "… stayed here to make sure all's well."

She gladly accepts the responsibility, takes the key and kisses Alex. The two together cooked a scrumptious chicken marsala dinner … late. Alex packed a small suitcase with his martial arts uniform, gear, and notes for the weekend. Then, they enjoyed a splendid midnight swim.

Christina: "So, since it's already so late, and you need me to give you a ride to work early in the morning, I kinda hafta spend the night here. But, I don't have a change of clothes." She shrugs.

"Well played, sir! I mean, … Sensei!"

Alex: "I shan't deny my being crafty, Sempai."

Christina: "On that note of your being my sensei, get over here!" She drags Alex into his bedroom and hip-tosses him onto his bed.

Alex: "Wowza! Fantastic. Oh gosh, sempai! Just for how amazing that was, I'll do twenty, … no, thirty, … no, fifty pushups!"

Alex feels so comfortable and not fatigued at fifty pushups, that he continues on, 'cuz he knows Christina likes his displays of strength. He aims for one hundred. But, he only gets to eighty-six. All those pushups worked up loads of perspiration.

Christina astutely observes the bodily fluids. "Alex, you're so sexy, when you're sweaty!"

Alex: "Really? Why the hell have I been showering all these years?"

Alex jumps in for another quicker shower. When he exits the bathroom, he finds Christina with a come hither look on her face—lying in his bed.

Christina: "I feel that we should celebrate your illustrious seminar with …" She winks.

Alex: "And, celebrate your acceptance of all my home

responsibilities! And, celebrate your technically being my fiancée!"

Christina giggles and blushes. She jumps out of Alex's bed, runs over to a still shower water-soaked Alex, jumps into his outstretched arms and nearly drowns him with a superfluity of sloppy kisses. Despite the lateness, the couple is energized by the obvious palpable affection. Alex's pleasantly surprised at how energetic Christina is at this late-night hour.

Alex quasi jokingly: "Okay, sempai. You get one free slap of my face just to wake me up, 'cuz I'm old."

Christina: "Okay. Yeeeeesss!"

She hurries over. She stands in front of him, winds up her right-hand way back and thrusts her upper body way forward. She stops her slap about two millimeters from Alex's face. Instead, she plants a kiss on his cheek and declares: "No, 'sen say'!"

The two slowly peel off each other's clothes, exchange kisses and climb into bed.

Christina: "Can I invite a friend or two over, while you're gone? To see my new house?"

He shrugs his shoulders. She massages 'em.

Alex: "Um, sure. Why not?"

Alex: "Before we begin, think about how sexy you said my wisdom is. 'Tis paramount to remember: If as you're discussing the immediate future, it instantly becomes the past. Thus, ...

There is no present!"

The couple make love all night, while listening to their song—Green River Ordinance's *Endlessly*—on repeat on Alex's laptop's speakers. In the morning, Christina grabs a small, older, workout tee of Alex's and three pairs of his shorts. She's gotta layer 'em, 'cuz they're big on her. To cover up. They share a delicious breakfast of baked apple pancakes and raspberries. Christina locks up the house and drives Alex to work.

EXCESSIVE HAPPINESS

At work Alex's got an extra spring in his step, 'cuz of his more than noteworthy romantic success! But he thinks to wait on sharing the spectacular news, 'til he buys a ring. So, he spends most—no, all—of his non movie time scouring the internet for reputable jewelers in the area. He finds one.

Alex rejoices with no one in particular. "Spectacular!"

He calls Christina to schedule when they'll get her ring.

"Babe, I found a jeweler for us to go pick out your ring. Can we go Sunday, when I get back? No, you'll prolly be too tired from the service. Monday?"

Christina: "Yay, honey! That'd be great. Monday it is."

Christina's just realizing the numerous things she's gotta do to prepare for her glorious day.

"What design do I want on my engagement ring? On our wedding rings? Who'll I invite to attend? Shorter list. Who won't I invite? Where should we celebrate? What father will marry us?"

Alex only has three movies to review today instead of his usual Friday of four films. Ya see, Alex had the foresight to know that he has to get out to catch his flight very soon after work. So, he critiques with Peter Simmons—Pocket Simon—today. The review duo crank out their three reviews without a problem. So, they depart for the airport.

Peter: "Ya got someone to pick you up, when you return?"

Alex: "Yeah, my fian …" He catches himself. "My girlfriend will get me on Sunday night."

So, Alex bobs and weaves through the airport traffic of people hurrying to their respective flights. Alex boards his flight in a timely manner. He can't sleep though, 'cuz he's far too excited about the soon to be…

"Mrs. … Christina Kalatovski".

"'Sempai … Christina Kalatovski".

"Co-homeowner … Christina Kalatovski".

Alex's on such an emotional high, that he doesn't notice how windy it has become outside.

Why would Alex notice? The wind is outside, and Alex's seated inside an airplane. The flight departs on time. For the first time ever, Alex brings musical entertainment with him anywhere! After Christina's wonderful entrance into his life, Alex always carries a small microchip with Green River Ordinance's *Endlessly* playing on repeat. The flight continues on without much of an alteration from the flight plan.

The flight goes smoothly for about forty-five minutes. Just then! The pilot announces on the plane's loudspeaker that, "The wind speed has reached approximately eighteen meters per second. Thaaat's— roughly— about forty miles per hour. So, it'll get pretty bumpy. Don't be alarmed. Just listen to the stewardesses tell you about safety precautions." Unfortunately, Alex's music's loud so he hears none of this.

Fortunately though, Alex keeps his eyes open. So, he witnesses the other passengers' starting to panic. He removes the song playing microchip to ask the gentleman across the aisle what the problem is.

"Winds! Bumpy! Losin' control! We're all gonna diiiiiiee!"

Okay, he did nothing to calm Alex's nerves. If anything, now Alex's jumpier than ever! The flight attendants quickly describe the safety procedures for seat cushions and oxygen tanks.

However, soon Alex hears a loud thud! Baaang! With his own supersonic hearing, Alex actually hears the pilot mutter, "That's not working! Oooooh, shit."

As the plane nosedives, Alex starts thinkin' about his comment to Christina. If as you're discussing the immediate future, it instantly becomes the past. Thus, there is no present! Thus, are we even here?"

He reattaches the microchip earplug, re-listens to his and Christina's song, closes his eyes and slowly chants, "Ooooooohmmmm." He's harnessing his qi in a final effort to become one.

THERE IN SPIRIT

Christina sleeps wonderfully that night in Alex's bed. She talks to herself aloud: "Thankfully, I transferred a few outfits over here last night. I do not think my kids would appreciate a naked minister!"

In her subconscious, Christina can hear Alex's retort: *Or, would they?*

Christina: "I've got to move the rest of my clothes into my new house."

On the way to her church for work, Christina's cell phone beeps with a news alert. Christina waits, to check the message. She gasps! Her heart nearly literally skips a beat. It states, "Delta flight #384 from Miami to Minneapolis crashed outside … near Atlanta. No survivors reported."

Christina gulps loudly. Her eyes moisten. She can't get out of her car. She plants her forehead on her steering wheel and bawls her eyes out. She thinks, *I know I've got a commitment to better educating these kids. But, there's no way I have the stable psyche to teach let alone talk. Right now! I should tell 'em.*

Christina—somehow—gathers the inner strength to push herself up and outta the car. She slowly trudges into the church. She barely has the energy to explain her awful position. Between long and loud tear deluges, Christina convinces the kids to call their parents for a ride home. She sincerely apologizes.

About an hour later, after all the kids leave Christina drives to her old home. She puts a bunch of her clothes and toiletries into a suitcase to bring to her new home.

"This'll be bag number one."

She guesstimates that she's got about eleven more suitcases worth of what-not to move. She sniffles a few times, before she grabs a tissue to blow her nose. After she loads up her suitcase into her car, she realizes just how heavy and time consuming all these satchel trips will be.

"Whom could I call to ask for help? Hhhmmm. … how 'bout Lisa's husband, Brandon?"

When Christina finally arrives at her new house, she starts exploring the house for interesting mementos of Alex's amazingness. She carefully walks through the living room. She finds a lot of Kalatovski family photos, many martial arts awards, even more film merchandise and notes. Then, she examines the kitchen. There's healthy food everywhere! Not like weird supplements and vitamin pills. Just nutritional foods! She finds chicken breasts, grapefruits, avocados, bananas, tons of eggs, almonds, asparagus, garlic, salmon and skim milk. The plethora of healthnut foods leave Christina flabbergasted.

"Jeez! Obsess much?"

Next, Christina checks out the Alex's bedroom. "I've been in here many a time. This won't be new."

But she is so wrong.

Christina decides to explore Alex's desktop computer.

"Oh, yeah! He had both a laptop and a desktop."

She finds numerous cinematic notes for work. She finds his martial arts notes for teaching and learning. She tears up when she sees that one song in his iTunes—*Endlessly* by Green River Ordinance. She cries loudly—yet smiles, when she reads the file label. "Our song."

As she scans Alex's desktop, Christina stumbles upon a semi hidden file. This is in his To-Do folder but attached to his obligations file. It's labelled "Marital vows."

Before she opens the document, Christina closes her eyes, inhales deeply, exhales audibly, and sheds a tear.

She repeats that breathing process six more times. She mumbles, "Open sesame."

Inside she finds maybe the most tear jerking words she's ever read. Ever.

Christina can't read it all without bawling uncontrollably, so she prints it. Having found the best memento, Christina shuts off the computer. She walks slowly to the printer to read the document.

I promise
To give as much as I can,
As often as I can,
Wherever I can,
However I can,
To you,
As my personal thank you, for rescuing me from my lonely rut.
That's 110 %.

As I am an anomaly, my affection does not follow the law of diminishing returns.

Don't question my math.

I couldn't have hoped for a more loyal, caring, attentive or attractive—inside and out—soulmate. All this time showed me was what I already knew about you. That you are always going to be there for me, and I hope I show you the same thing. I may not always tell you. But, I will always show you, just how much I adore you.

I am not perfect—by any stretch of the imagination! To give y'all a reference point, I'm somewhere between a pronghorn antelope and a gazelle. ... And a sailfish.

Alas, neither are you perfect. Damn close, though! But, we are... Perfect for each other!

Throughout your life, remember: try to leave a mark. Choose thine mark appropriately.

Finally, I must ask: "What do you do, when you realize you've gotten all you want in life?"

Personally, I'd marry her. Sooo, Check.

You must form your own destiny with me!"

Reading Alex's marital words really initiated Christina's thought processing.

How long must I mourn? In lieu of my loved one's untimely death, I'm really questioning my career and its accompanying faith. How could I best commemorate Alex's amazing effect on my life?

Christina sleeps well that night, ... except for the ... one, ... two, ... four different times she awoke to cry. She decides that there's no way she could attend a service.

Lasting Effect

Christina awakens in a terrible mood. Well, I suppose that's understandable, considering her current situation—recently perished fiancé and a newly doubtful faith. The very first thing that Christina does that Sunday morning is retrieve those worry beads that Alex gave her.

"Wow, I'm really worryin' now! But, how could I always have this gift to ease my concerns?"

Christina calls upon her girl scout skills from way back when to morph her worry beads into a necklace. Christina chokes up to state—with a grin, "God bless Alex for teaching me that the circumference—or distance around a circle—is equal to π times diameter. Or π times twice the radius. Christina feels this subconscious urge to push back her imaginary glasses—like a nerd—despite her 20/20 vision. She knows that that's Alex's doing. So, she giggles, surprisingly snorts, points upward to heaven, blows a kiss and whispers, "Thanks, babe."

She transforms the bead string into a choker necklace. Christina does the sign of the cross, kisses her first two fingers and glances heavenward.

"I promise to keep you in my mind 24-7 by never removing these beads."

Again, Christina tears up.

"God, how could you take away such a wonderful gift? Not just from me, but from all these kids in martial arts?"

She deeply and audibly inhales a big breath. "I'll do it. I'll accept your classes as your *sempai*. Of course, I'll still need alotta help … for all the moves and techniques and fighting principles. But, I'll get it."

Christina occupies all of her Sunday with multiple back and forth trips—with Brandon—to move all her stuff into her new house. Finally, after just six more transfer trips, Christina has all her stuff in her new house.

Christina: "Thanks a ton, Brandon! You are a phenomenal packer."

Brandon: "No prob, Christina. Alex used to say that I could pack the square peg into the circle hole. Ha ha!"

Christina: "Brandon. Might you, perchance, know how to get to Alex's movie job? I wanna clean up a few things."

Brandon explains and writes down how to get there.

So, Christina redecorates her house with a clearly more feminine and less martial arts obsessed motif. Exhausted, she falls asleep in her bed. She only wakes up twice to cry. Sooooo, … yaaay! Seeing as Christina's not used to this work week's starting on Mondays at 8 AM hoopla, she sleeps until brunch. She arises and hears that she has an email. Christina smiles, as her eyes water, and she reads, "Congratulations! Welcome to house ownership!

As I'm sure you've discussed with Alex, he's added you as 'co owner'. There are no house payments for rent. But, copies of all monthly bills and announcements will be carbon copied to you."

Christina is so proud of and amazed with her man.

"Jeez! What didn't he think of?"

So, Christina wanders into Alex's film review work, explains his horrendous and tragic downfall—pun intended—who she is and asks whether she can apply for a job. Since Alex was, by far, his most responsible employee, the company owner gives her the job—on a temporary trial basis.

"Your first assignment is … the 1975 classic, *One Flew Over the*

Cuckoo's Nest."

Christina bravely steps into one of Alex's black belt only workouts and asks for help with teaching. She gets three volunteers.

Finally, Christina grows the stones to tell her church, that she's accepted a new, non-theological occupation.

Christina to her church's main priest: "'Twas an instrumental delight to teach and learn all these years. But…" She sniffles. "I've found a new calling!"

Afterword

The preceding tale was (roughly) my life plan for my first and only—as of yet—true love. I (erroneously) thought my love was symbiotic and mutual. But, after almost five years of living together, she still inexplicably blew an emotional fuse and left my severely damaged mind utterly bamboozled as to why she ended her happiness. As she never explained her ludicrous and warped thinking, I can only try to be the logical, caring and understanding man who I am, and give her the benefit of the doubt.

Ergo, my often confused head thinks she's been having personal issues and family problems for … over six years. But, my spiteful heart feels she's bonkers and mean. Nevertheless, my ambivalence inspired my nonstop writing.

ABOUT THE AUTHOR

Since the age of ~114 months (~9.5 years), the author's been a bit of a math prodigy. He taught himself how to multiply double digit numbers in his head. But, unfortunately, he can't write his memoirs quantitatively. So, just please bear with him, as he admirably tries to use these ... What do you call 'em?! ... Words.

Connect with AJ on social media.

Or on the web at www.tbiauthor.com

Made in the USA
Columbia, SC
22 December 2019